LADY GUNSMITH

Roxy Doyle and the Christmas Gift

Books by J.R. Roberts
(Robert J. Randisi)

Lady Gunsmith Series
The Legend of Roxy Doyle
The Three Graves of Roxy Doyle
Roxy Doyle and The Shanghai Saloon
Roxy Doyle and The Traveling Circus Show
The Portrait of Gavin Doyle
Roxy Doyle and the Desperate Housewife
Roxy Doyle and the James Boys
Roxy Doyle and the Silver Queen
Roxy Doyle and the Lady Executioner
Roxy Doyle Meets an Angel

The Gunsmith Series

Gunsmith Giant Series

Angel Eyes Series

Tracker Series

Mountain Jack Pike Series

For more information visit:
www.SpeakingVolumes.us

LADY GUNSMITH

Roxy Doyle and the Christmas Gift

J.R. Roberts

SPEAKING VOLUMES, LLC
NAPLES, FLORIDA
2023

Roxy Doyle and the Christmas Gift

Copyright © 2023 by Robert J. Randisi

ISBN 979-8-89022-068-4

Chapter One

Omaha, NE

Roxy Doyle had never seen anything so beautiful.

Samuel Dunham smiled as he gently laid the necklace across the redhead's palm.

"Sixteen perfect diamonds around the outside of a gold heart with a two carat ruby in the center. It was my mother's."

Roxy touched the turquoise piece hanging on her hat that had belonged to her own mother. No one could understand the significance of Sam's family heirloom as well as she could.

The gold heart caught the light as Sam picked it up. "And now it's going to belong to Violet, my daughter. A special gift for her tenth Christmas."

"She'll love it," Roxy told him as he carefully put it back in its velvet box. "Any girl would love it."

Sam set the box on the table next to his bed, then rolled over and kissed Roxy's shoulder.

"The only problem is getting it to her."

"Lincoln's only a day's ride. If you left early enough—"

"That's the problem," he interrupted, "I can't go."

"Well," she started, "Christmas is a week off. You could go—"

"I can't go anytime. Her mother is now married to the sheriff. The two of 'em have it in for me. I can't step foot in town let alone see my daughter." He fell back on his pillow.

Roxy cursed Sam Dunham's handsome face. His blue eyes had been the first thing she noticed when they'd met. And when he invited her to supper, she eagerly accepted, surprising herself more than him. Supper led to a drink in his hotel room. As he told her about himself, she only half-listened, too intent on watching his mouth. When he finally kissed her, Roxy held on tight until she had to have him and started tearing at his shirt.

"Why, Miss Doyle, what do you think you're doing?"

"Shut up. You talk too much."

She pulled at the belt around his waist. Sam didn't really put up much of a fight. When he was finally completely naked, his cock stiff, he pulled her blouse, yanked off her belt and threw her on the bed while taking off the rest of his own clothes. The frenzy between them grew until he was on top of her, desperate to get inside, each jerk making her wetter.

Roxy couldn't get enough of him. Neither one slowed down. Sam rode her until the sheets were wet with her juices. Then he held her up and laid down beneath her.

Crouching on top of him, she bounced frantically while he gripped her hips, pulling her down harder each time. They took a moment to catch their breath, kissing loudly, then Sam pushed his fingers between Roxy's legs up inside her, rubbing until she couldn't take it anymore.

"I've never known a woman like you," he whispered.

She only laughed. Men had told her that before, but she never really believed them.

When she went limp, collapsing onto the bed next to him, he started kissing her breasts. The gentle nuzzles soon became bites, starting their passion up again . . .

* * *

For two days they stayed locked in that room, only stopping to eat a quick meal they'd ordered up from the kitchen. On day three Sam talked about the necklace again.

"I know a trip to Lincoln wasn't in your plans, but I was kind of hoping that maybe . . . ." He smiled at her, those beautiful eyes of his sparkling in a way that could make her say and do anything he asked. "Maybe you could take it to Violet for me."

"But we only just met. I don't even know your daughter, or your wife."

"She's not my wife anymore," he snapped.

"Why me?"

"You're Lady Gunsmith," he said. "An intimidating woman. Strong. A man would think twice before coming against you. And I trust you."

Roxy smiled. "You don't think I'll just hightail it and take off with your necklace?"

"I'm a real good judge of character," he said. "We've been together now for two days."

"Three," she said, knowing she sounded like a silly, lovesick woman.

He reached out and hugged her. "I'm starving. Let's go find someplace to have breakfast."

"We *have* worked up an appetite. Give me a minute to get dressed."

As she bent down to gather her clothes, he playfully smacked her butt.

Chapter Two

They spotted the Bread Basket at the same time.

"Must have great food; the place is so crowded," Roxy said.

The waiter motioned for them to find a table, but the only empty ones were near the large front window.

Sam started to sit but Roxy stood, looking uncomfortable.

"What's wrong?" he asked. "Why don't you sit down?"

Clint Adams, the Gunsmith, had pounded it into her head that she should always sit in the back of a public room, away from eyes that might be looking to challenge her. Once she'd chosen the gunfighter's life, she'd also had to accept the restrictions. No matter how taken she was with Sam Dunham, she couldn't forget Clint's rules.

But maybe just this once . . .

Before she could explain herself, a table in the back was suddenly cleared and ready. "Let's sit back there." She pointed. "That way we can have some privacy."

"Sure thing." Sam stood up and followed her to the back table.

A waiter came rushing over, holding a coffee pot and two cups.

"Looks like everyone in town wants breakfast at the same time this morning. I'll be with you folks in a minute." After setting the coffee down in the middle of their table, he pulled two menus from under his arm and hurried off.

"Is coffee okay?" Sam asked, amused. "We can always get you something else when he runs back over here."

"Coffee's fine," she said, opening her menu.

Roxy felt as though she could eat one of everything. Sex with Sam had been unbelievable, but now she needed food, and a lot of it.

"Sorry," their waiter said when he returned with his pad and pencil ready to take their order. "Never seen it like this before."

"Something special happening in town?" Sam asked.

"Just folks getting ready for the holidays, visiting relatives, that sort of thing. Now, what'll you have?"

She'd had enough of the chit-chat and was tired of listening to her stomach rumbling.

"Three eggs over easy, toast with lots of butter, bacon, potatoes, and preserves for the toast if you have some . . ."

"Fresh biscuits if you'd like them instead of toast," the waiter said.

"Sure, but I still want the toast."

Sam sat with his mouth open while Roxy ordered enough food to feed several more people. When there was a pause, Sam told the waiter he just wanted eggs and bacon, thinking he'd help Roxy eat some of her order.

While they waited for their breakfast, Sam fidgeted. In the daylight, out of bed, he seemed awkward, not the self-assured lover she'd been so taken with.

"You must get told how beautiful you are all the time?"

"Not all the time," she kidded.

"When I walked into that saloon, you were the only thing I noticed. Your hair, red like a flame."

"And so you had to meet me, right?"

"Oh, I knew who you were. The whole town's been buzzin' since you arrived."

Thinking back to that night, Roxy remembered introducing herself and his surprise. Maybe he didn't want to appear cocky. Maybe he was nervous.

"And what did you think of me?" he asked.

"Well, I'm sure women tell you how handsome you are, because you look like you could be on the stage."

He smiled. "I traveled with a theater group in my youth. But when they disbanded, I went back to Ohio. That's where I met Julie—Violet's mother. She worked in her family's bakery."

"How did you ever end up in Nebraska?" she asked.

"After Violet was born, we decided to come out West. Julie's folks came out last Spring. They opened up a bakery in Lincoln; Julie manages the operation."

"And you worked there, too?" Roxy asked.

"No, I did . . . odd jobs." When the waiter came by to leave the bill, Sam took his turn to ask questions. "So what brings you to Nebraska? I don't remember hearing anything about you living out this way."

"I've been traveling a lot recently, looking for my father. Maybe you've heard of Gavin Doyle? He's a bounty hunter."

Sam thought for a moment. "The name sounds familiar. Could be I read about him."

"Maybe. I've run into a lot of people who've known him."

"How long you been looking?"

"A few years. My mother died when I was little. My father left me with a family and took off. That was a long time ago."

"Are you sure he's still alive?" Sam asked.

"Very sure." All of a sudden Roxy's stomach was full and she laid down her fork.

"If you take that necklace to Violet, I could help you look for your dad. Consider it my way of thanking you."

The idea of having his company on the trail was very appealing.

"How long could you be away?" she asked.

"A few weeks, I guess. Maybe more." He reached out and ran his fingers lightly over her left hand as it laid on top of the table.

"That would be nice." Her heart raced as he continued to touch her.

"So when can you leave for Lincoln? The sooner, the better."

"I'll go tomorrow."

Chapter Three

That night Sam slept in Roxy's room at The Prairie House Hotel.

"We'll have breakfast together before you leave," he told her. "You'll need plenty of energy for the ride."

She'd been traveling alone for a few years and knew very well how to take care of herself. But the attention felt good, and she agreed with his plans. When they got into bed, however, he didn't seem very concerned about using up some of her energy to please both of them beneath the sheets.

* * *

Sam walked with her to the stable at the end of the street. The hostler brought her Morgan outside.

"Pretty animal," the heavyset man said, patting the horse's rump. "What's her name?"

"I don't know," Roxy said. "Bought her at an auction in Kansas City. No sense in naming an animal like a person."

"A good horse can be your best friend," the stranger told her. "Why, I've heard tell of a golden Palomino who saved his owner, ran miles to bring help to the poor man in the desert. I'm sure you can come up with a good name while you're getting to know her better."

"Maybe," Roxy said, but she wasn't sure it would happen.

"Well," Sam said, as he helped her into the saddle, "I'll be here waiting when you get back. If everything goes right, you'll be back on Friday." Holding up the jewelry box wrapped in brown paper, he stuck it deep into her saddlebag. "Violet's address is inside, along with the necklace. Thanks again for doing this, Roxy. I'll spend weeks thanking you."

He reached up, pulled her face close to his and kissed her goodbye.

* * *

The wind was chilly, the ground hard as the sun was slowly rising. By the time she was out of town, past houses and shops, she was happy she'd agreed to make the trip to Lincoln. She could always breathe easier in open spaces. And knowing she was bringing a special gift from a father to his daughter would be a Christmas memory Roxy would treasure.

If only her own father had sent her a Christmas present or just a letter to keep her updated of his whereabouts. So many years spent chasing stories and legends of the famous bounty hunter, Gavin Doyle, had left her frustrated and sad. Sometimes she just wanted to give up. If he cared about her at all, wouldn't he have looked for her?

Wasn't finding people what he did?

As the day wore on, the temperature dropped slightly. By noon, even though the wind had died down, the sun didn't seem to warm her. She led her horse to a large pine tree, tied her securely and climbed down from the saddle. The waiter had made up a sandwich from leftover bread and bacon they had eaten for breakfast. Sitting on the ground, Roxy unwrapped her lunch and glanced at the Morgan. The animal nibbled on some grass but looked at the bacon sandwich longingly.

"I have a few apples for you," Roxy told the animal. "That'll be your lunch. This is mine."

The horse sniffed loudly.

When the last bite of bread was gone, Roxy walked over to the horse and fed her two apples and poured some water from her canteen into the tin cup she had also packed.

Something cold fell on her cheek. A light snow drifted down. Roxy felt around inside her saddlebag for the wool scarf she kept at the bottom. Wrapping it around her neck then tucking the fringed ends inside her jacket, she pulled herself up into the saddle.

The snow came down heavier as she rode the last ten miles toward Lincoln. It packed beneath her horse's hoofs, causing her to slip and slide every so often. When they rode into town it was dark and frigid. All Roxy had been thinking about for two hours was a warm bed and lots of sleep.

Luckily the stable near what looked like a decent hotel had a lamp glowing inside. She dropped down to the hay sprinkled in front of the large double doors and guiding her horse, knocked.

"Hello! Anyone there?"

She stood, shivering, waiting for what seemed like ten minutes but probably was only a few. Then she knocked again, this time with both fists.

"Hold on!" came a gruff voice from inside. "I'm comin'."

The doors finally swung open and a middle-aged man with so much black hair that he looked like a bear, stood there.

"Do you have any idea what time . . ." The hostler stopped abruptly while he took in the sight of Roxy Doyle.

Having to soothe ruffled feathers of men her entire life, Roxy knew how to handle someone like this man.

"I'm so sorry but I just got into town. My horse and I need to get warm and find some food. Thank goodness you were inside." She smiled.

"No problem, Miss. I live in the back." He reached for the reins. "Here, let me help."

The inside of the stable was warm and clean. Every stall was occupied. A few of the horses whinnied but most seemed disinterested.

"We're full up, what with Christmas bein' a few days off, relatives come to town to celebrate with their kinfolk. But I got a special place in the back where I usually keep Bob, that's my own animal. Lucky for you my son borrowed him for the week."

"This is so kind of you," Roxy said. "I'm only planning on being in town for a day or two—no more."

"No matter, Miss . . ."

"Doyle. Roxy Doyle."

"You know, I thought I recognized you from the pictures I seen. As if all that red hair wouldn't give you away." He winked.

"And you are?" she asked.

"Binder. Woodrow Binder. But you can call me Woody."

She reached out to shake the man's hand.

"Well, thank you for your kindness, Woody. Now if you can tell me the name of the closest hotel, I'll get out of your hair."

"At the end of the block," he said, "the Baron House. Tell 'em I sent you. Everybody in town knows me."

"I'll do that," Roxy said.

She started for the doors when Woody called out to her. "What's your animal's name?"

"No name," Roxy called over her shoulder.

But Woody heard, " 'Nona.' "

Chapter Four

"I knew it! I told you that was her!" Stony whispered to Vernon.

"What the hell is the Lady Gunsmith doing here?" Vernon asked.

"How should I know? I just hope she don't screw up our plans."

Vernon spit out a mouthful of tobacco. "You think she could do that?"

"Her daddy's some kinda lawman. Maybe he got wind of what we was plannin' and told her."

The two men had been hiding in the shadows behind the barn ever since spotting Roxy ride into town.

"Why would she care about the likes of us?" Vernon asked.

Stony shrugged. "Beats the hell outta me. But we still gotta be careful. Can't let our guard down for one minute."

"Careful. Right, Stony."

* * *

With her saddlebags over her shoulder, Roxy started walking toward The Baron House. Snow was starting to pile up along the street. She thought it would be wise to get a room for a few days, not just one night. That would give her time to find out more about Sam Dunham and his daughter. And hopefully, the snow would let up enough for her to ride back to Omaha safely.

Pine wreaths decorated with red and green glass ornaments had been hung on every lamppost. Several of the shops along Main Street were still open, she could see a clerk in the toy store wrapping something in shiny paper. She remembered the last Christmas her family had spent together, before her Mama died. Her father tried to keep up the traditions, but his heart was broken, and he started drinking. When he couldn't take the pain, he left his little girl with a family he thought he could trust and rode away never learning of the abuse Roxy had suffered. But that last Christmas with him had been perfect and the memory of the joy and warmth sustained her through many sad times.

A man with a small cart was selling something. As she got closer, he held out a paper bag filled with warm chestnuts to her.

"No thanks," Roxy said as she kept walking.

"No charge, Miss. They're my last batch. Please, take them so I can go home."

Roxy smiled. "That's very kind of you, thanks."

"And a Happy Christmas to you and yours."

When he smiled, Roxy could see he was missing a few of his front teeth.

* * *

The lobby of The Baron House was warm and inviting. A large fireplace took up almost an entire wall of the grand room. In the corner was a Christmas tree covered with paper ornaments and popcorn garlands. Candles placed on small tables burned. She felt as though she'd walked into a Currier and Ives lithograph. Taking in the glorious scene, Roxy was startled when a voice called her from across the room.

"Miss! Can I help you?"

She turned to see a distinguished looking man behind a shiny mahogany counter.

"Oh, sorry." Roxy walked over to the register. "Your lobby is so pretty."

"Thank you, my wife decorated." The man said proudly.

"Well, please give her my compliments."

"I'll be sure to do that. Now, may I ask if you have a reservation?"

"I'm not sure."

"Well, with the holidays and all, I'm afraid . . ."

"I was hoping a friend of mine, Samuel Dunham, made a reservation for me."

The man spun the register around and ran his finger down the list of names.

"Sorry, no. We don't have anything for a Mr. Dunham or his guest. And your name would be? . . ."

"Roxy Doyle."

"Oh, the Lady Gunsmith? Oh my." He spoke nervously. "Why, you know we always set aside a room for just such a situation. A special room, for a special guest." He winked.

"That's very kind, but I'm not special. A simple room will do. I just need clean sheets and a soft bed."

Without hesitating, the man reached out and hit the bell at his elbow.

"Harry will be right over to help you with your belongings."

Before she could object, a muscular man scurried over and grabbed the saddlebags from Roxy's shoulder.

"Allow me, Miss."

"Harry, take Miss Doyle to the third floor. Number five."

Harry's eyebrows shot up. "Okay, boss."

Roxy was too tired to argue, and after thanking the clerk she followed Harry to the staircase.

When they stopped in front of number five, Harry opened the door with the key he had been holding.

"After you, Miss."

Roxy had stayed in some fancy hotels, but this room was elegant. Through the sitting room door she could see a bedroom with a canopy bed. Cream colored satin covered the settee and two matching chairs. The walls were covered in green floral paper. Gold frames held nature scenes.

"Did the clerk's wife decorate this room, too?" she asked.

"He's not just a clerk," Harry said. "That's Mr. Clark, he owns and runs the Baron House. His wife is Matilda."

"Well, I'll be sure to pass along my compliments when I go down tomorrow."

"They'll like that," Harry said. "They both take such pride in the place."

"Well, it shows," Roxy said.

After carefully laying the saddlebags on one of the chairs, Harry asked if there was anything else Roxy needed.

"No, everything's just fine, thanks."

"If you're around tomorrow, you should go down to the park, it's just a few blocks south of here. There's gonna be a Christmas fair. Food, games and don't tell anyone but Santa's makin' a special visit. We got a real good one this time. Last year's St. Nick was drunk by the time the kids arrived."

"Sounds like fun. Maybe I'll have a look."

She was thinking about asking Harry if he knew Sam Dunham or his wife, Julie, but was too tired to have a lengthy conversation. It would have to wait for the morning.

"Okay then, I'll be downstairs if you need anything."

"All I need now is some sleep," Roxy said.

Chapter Five

The snow was falling in clumps the next day, landing in Roxy's hair, dripping down the collar of her coat as she walked. After having breakfast, she decided to explore Lincoln and hopefully, learn a little more about Sam Dunham. When she saw the sign for Wilson's Bakery, she remembered Sam telling her that his ex-wife ran a family business and hoped it was the right one.

As she got closer, she could see Christmas cookies and a large gingerbread house displayed in the window. When she opened the door, a blast of warm air hit her face and the scent of fresh bread drifted up her nose.

"May I help you?" a man asked.

"Are you the owner?" she asked.

"Only through marriage." He smiled. "My wife and her family own the shop; I just help out now and then."

Roxy was sure she had the right place when she spotted the sheriff's badge shining beneath the man's apron. But the new husband didn't want Sam seeing Violet. She had to think how she could get the necklace to the girl without causing trouble.

"I'll have half a dozen of those," she pointed to the butter cookies.

"That I can do." He smiled and put the cookies into a small brown paper bag.

"I heard there's a party in the park," she said as she dug in her pocket for money to pay for the cookies.

"Oh, you mean the fair. My wife's over there right now setting things up. But the festivities won't start until after the kids are out of school. Around four, if you're interested."

"I might just go over there."

"Mind if I ask what brings you to town?" the sheriff asked.

Taking a chance she said, "I'm just passing through on my way to Omaha. My friend, Samuel Dunham, told me what a fine town Lincoln is." She waited for a reaction.

"You're a friend of Sam's, huh? And stopping at Julie's shop was just a coincidence? I suppose you're gonna tell me you didn't know my wife and your friend used to be married?"

"To tell the truth, I forgot until I saw the bakery."

"Just how well do you know Mr. Dunham?" the man asked angrily.

"Is he wanted?" Roxy asked. "Has he broken any laws?"

"No. Being a scoundrel isn't against the law."

"I understand you'd want to protect your wife from any harm. But what happened between the two of them isn't anyone's concern . . ."

"So, I'm just supposed to sit back and watch him neglect his fatherly duties and insult the woman I love?"

Before things got worse, Roxy decided to leave.

"Forgive me for interfering. I meant no disrespect."

"No, I'm too hot-headed," the man said. "A bad thing to be when you're a sheriff. But Julie has the scars to remember ole Sam by. If I catch him near my family . . ."

The bell over the front door rang as an elderly woman walked in.

"Hey, Lloyd. Got any of those cinnamon buns left?" When she saw Roxy, she stopped. "Oh, I didn't know you had a customer."

Roxy smiled and held up her bag. "I was just leaving."

* * *

Stony and Vernon walked out of the doorway across the street from the bakery. They quickly fell behind Roxy, trying to maintain a safe distance. When she walked past the Baron House, they were confused.

"Where's she goin' now?" Vernon whined. "Come on, Stony, I'm cold and hungry. We got hours til things liven up. Plenty of time to warm up at Bertha's."

"We ain't goin' to no saloon right now. We gotta get ready for later."

"And why does the job have to be later?" Vernon asked. "The streets are quiet, no one's goin' in or out of the bank. The time is perfect. Especially with that damn sheriff servin' up cakes an' pies."

"We follow orders. Hank's a lot smarter than us. That means he knows real good what he's doin'," Stony said.

"I know, I know. But—"

"You want to spend the rest of your days in jail? Or even worse—hanged?" Stony grunted.

"No. I do not."

When the two men looked up, Roxy had disappeared. They quickly turned onto the side street that ran along the hotel and bumped into Roxy Doyle, her colt pointed at them.

"Stop right there! Both of you!" she shouted.

The two men froze.

"We ain't done nothin'," Vernon told her. "You got no right pointin' your weapon at us."

"And you have no right following me. Did you think I wouldn't notice you two no-goods stumbling on my heels?" Roxy asked.

"She's good, Stony," Vernon looked across his right shoulder at his partner.

"So I've heard," Stony mumbled.

"Who told you about me?" Roxy demanded.

Stony and Vernon stood there, tight-lipped.

"Looks like I'll have to coax a name out of you," Roxy said.

"Think you're so smart, bitch?" Vernon demanded. "Think a dumb-ass woman can go up against two men?"

"Yes, I do," Roxy said. "Especially when those men are idiots."

"Why I oughta . . ." Vernon started as he raised his hand.

Before he could finish his threat, Roxy shot Vernon's hat off.

"Aww, look what you done. An' it's my favorite. Hank'll show you . . ."

"Shut-up, you fool," Stony snapped.

"Hank?" Roxy asked. "Who's Hank? Your boss? Gotta be, cause you two don't seem capable of having a smart idea between you." She smiled, hoping her remark hit their egos.

"Now hold on there," Stony started. "We ain't done nothin' to you 'cept follow you down a street. We ain't laid one finger on the precious Lady Gunsmith. We was just out for a stroll. Ain't no law against that, is there?"

He had her. Neither of the men had threatened or hurt her.

"Pick up that sorry hat of yours and get away from me," she told Vernon. "If you follow me again, I'll go to the sheriff."

Vernon laughed as he brushed the snow off his hat. "The sheriff here sells baked goods. He don't have no time to go after bad guys."

Stony grabbed his partner's arm. "Shut your damn mouth, will ya?" he grumbled. Then he dragged Vernon toward the nearest saloon.

Chapter Six

Roxy ate a few butter cookies as she walked toward the park. Signs flapping in the cold breeze announced that Santa Claus would be coming to the fair. A brightly colored illustration showed the jolly man in a long red coat, trimmed in white fur, a matching hat, on top of his head. He was holding a small Christmas tree and at his feet was a sack filled with toys.

Hoping Violet Dunham would be among the children in the park, Roxy suddenly realized she didn't know how she would recognize the child. As she wondered what to do next, she remembered that Clint Adams told her once to be direct.

Booths were set up in a large circle. Each had a sign declaring what was being sold. A short woman struggled to tie a banner with the name WILSON over her booth. Roxy hurried over to help her.

"Let me hold that for you," she told the woman.

"Thank you so much. Everyone else is too busy to notice me. Wish my husband was here. He's the tall one in our marriage."

When the two women finally got the sign in place, Roxy stood back to admire the hand-painted picture showing a loaf of bread, fresh from the oven.

"You run the bakery in town?" she asked.

"Yes, Wilson's Bakery. Well, my parents own it, but I run it now that they're older." The woman smiled. "Thanks so much for your help. I'm Julie Dunham. And you are?"

"Roxy Doyle."

She reached for the bag she had set in the snow. Holding it up she told the woman about visiting her shop and complimented her on the wonderful cookies.

"Then you must have met my husband, Lloyd. He's helping out today."

It was obvious Julie wasn't aware of Roxy's reputation.

"Sheriff Dunham, right?" Roxy asked.

"No, Dunham's my—was—my married name. I kept it so's not to confuse Violet, my daughter. There's always time to go to the courthouse and do the paperwork later, when she's older."

"Is your ex-husband living here in town?" Roxy asked.

"No, he's in Omaha."

"So Violet doesn't get to see him very often?"

Julie made a face. "If I had my way, she'd never see him again. My marriage didn't end on a good note."

Before Roxy could get more information out of the woman, a pretty girl with long blonde hair walked over to them.

"Do you think Santa will come to the park, Mama?"

"I don't know, honey" Julie said and winked at Roxy.

"I'm hungry," the child whined.

Roxy offered one of her cookies.

"Can I?" Violet asked.

Her mother nodded. "Thank Miss Doyle."

"Thank you, Miss Doyle," the girl said.

As Violet ate her cookie, Roxy studied her face. She had Sam's blue eyes and strong jaw. Her skin was smooth as satin, and Roxy liked her immediately. But would she be upsetting Violet by mentioning her father?

Squeals suddenly ran through the crowd as a sleigh glided across the snow and a fat man wearing a red suit pulled the reins, bringing the two horses to a halt.

"Santa! He's here!" Violet screamed. Before her mother could stop her, Violet ran with the other children to greet Santa.

"Your daughter's very pretty," Roxy told Julie. "I envy you having such a darling child. I imagine she's a daddy's girl?"

"Unfortunately, yes. But maybe when she's older she'll realize what an awful man he is."

"Awful?"

"He's violent. I had to grab Violet and run away from him before he hurt her."

"Guess I was lucky," Roxy said. "My father was a kind man."

"So was mine," Julie said. "But then I found Lloyd. He's just about the best man I've ever known."

Their conversation was interrupted by shouts from the excited children, now gathered around Santa.

"I hope we meet again, Miss Doyle, but now I have to go tend to Violet."

"Of course," Roxy said and watched as the anxious mother ran to her child.

How could she have been so wrong about Sam Dunham? The man she knew was funny and the best lover she'd ever had. In the days they'd spent together there hadn't been one glimmer of a mean streak behind those warm eyes. And never once had a cruel or malicious word passed his lips. Had she been too wrapped up in their lovemaking to notice his true nature?

A small tent was set up across the park. Painted with red letters a large sign had been placed on top. HOT CIDER AND COCOA it advertised. Roxy headed over to get something to warm up. Along the way she passed

Santa Claus who was talking to an older boy. Then the jolly man reached out and gently patted the child on the back.

"Be good and take care, now!" he called after him.

The exact words her own father had said to her every day of the few years she'd had him to herself.

Roxy stopped abruptly.

Then she asked the question she'd asked him every day. "Take care of what?"

"My little girl," Gavin Doyle said. "Take real good care of my little girl, Roxanne."

Chapter Seven

David Cherry Middleton was a horse thief from Arizona. He moved around a lot, trying his hand at different occupations. One day he was a saloon keeper, the next a farmer. But honest work didn't seem to suit him and soon his laziness won out. Running livestock off the range and selling what he could for profit, stealing horses taught him it was far easier to break the law than follow it. And much more profitable.

His name changed as often as his hometown. One day he was David Middleton, the next Henry Shepherd or Henry Riley, whichever served him best. But for now he was living in Nebraska under the name, Henry Shepherd.

With each year that passed, Henry—his cohorts called him Hank—realized he couldn't continue the way he had in his youth. Famous outlaws like the James gang didn't mess around with two-bit jobs. Robbing banks was where the big money was, and Hank wanted some of that big money. So, he planned to rob the First National Bank of Lincoln in the winter when the trail would be packed with snow and ice. That way a posse would be slowed down. And with everyone in town occupied with their Christmas party, no one would ever notice if Hank and his gang made a large withdrawal. He'd thought of everything—made the perfect plan. An easy in and out, no bloodshed.

But then Lady Gunsmith showed up.

* * *

"Daddy?" Roxy asked the man dressed as Santa Claus. "Is that really you?"

St. Nick's eyes widened. "Roxanne? Is that you?"

Quickly he jumped out of the sled and grabbed her into a bear hug.

Having her father there, in her arms, was more wonderful than she could have imagined. He smelled of pipe tobacco and pine. His warm hug comforted her, and she fought off the tears burning her eyes.

After a minute Doyle broke his embrace and held his daughter at arm's length.

"My, my, you certainly have grown into a beautiful woman." The pride in his voice was evident. "And from what I hear, you've made quite a reputation for yourself."

"If you heard about me, you must have known I've been looking for you. Why did you keep running away? It's been years, Dad."

"I wasn't running away from you, sweetheart. Never would I run away from my baby girl. I made sure you were safe and with a good family when I left . . ."

"They were horrible people. That's why I ran away. The only thing I wanted to do was find you, be with you."

She couldn't hold the hurt back and started to cry.

A few children wandered over to see Santa, pulling at the hem of his coat.

"This isn't the right time to have our talk," Doyle told Roxy. "Tell me where you're staying and when I'm done here, I'll come over for a nice heart-to-heart. Okay?"

After wiping away some of the tears on her cheek, Roxy gave Doyle the name of her hotel. They agreed on a time later that evening. As excited as she was, somewhere in Roxy's heart was the fear that he wouldn't show, and she'd lose him again. If what he said was true, that he wasn't running away from her, there must have been something else he was running from. She was determined to know what it was.

* * *

"Now ain't that just about the strangest sight you ever did see?" Stony asked. "The famous Lady Gunsmith talkin' to Santa Claus?"

Vernon nodded. "It surely is."

"And I do believe she's cryin' now. What's got her so choked up?"

"Maybe Santa don't have the toy she wanted." Vernon nudged his partner and laughed at his own joke.

Stony pushed Vernon away from him.

"No time for jokes, fool. Hank's comin' tonight, sometime after supper. We'll meet up at Big Bertha's to hear the plan."

"So we're pullin' the job tonight?" Vernon asked. "For sure?"

"Nothin's for sure until we talk to Hank. Now come on. Looks like our lady over there ain't gonna give us any trouble. Not with Santa around to keep her busy."

The two men turned away and headed for the saloon.

* * *

Roxy unpacked her clothes, laying out her finest blouse. The sleeves were trimmed in blue lace, her father's favorite color. When she took out a pair of clean jeans, the necklace Sam had given her fell out and landed on the bed. In her excitement to see her father, she realized she'd forgotten all about the gift for Violet Dunham. Picking up the jewelry box she opened it to study the beautiful necklace. It sparkled in the light from the lamp on the small bedside table. Yes, it was just as lovely as she remembered.

She debated a moment if she should keep it with her or leave it behind in the room, when she went out for dinner. There were still a few hours until dark and the Fair would be shut down for the night. Slowly she walked around her room, looking for a hiding place for the present. As she stood thinking, the large painting of a summer landscape, behind her bed, caught her attention. Walking over to it, she lifted it away from the wall and saw the frame had wires holding the picture in place. Inside her saddlebag were several pairs of wool stockings. She took out one, put the necklace deep in the toe and rolled the stocking around the box. Then she wedged the whole thing behind the wires until it was secure. Releasing the frame, the painting fell into place, flat against the wall.

As Roxy finished unpacking, she kept looking at the painting above the bed to make sure nothing was out of place. When she was satisfied, she stretched out across the bed for a nap.

Chapter Eight

It was dark when Roxy woke. A small clock near her bed chimed seven times. She peered out her window which overlooked the main street. Normally, she would have made sure her room didn't overlook the street, but there was no access from outside, and the building across the street was only one floor.

Drunk cowhands, probably in town for the holiday, were shouting and carrying on in front of a saloon. Horses trotted by, children ran, throwing snowballs at each other. Every time one hit its target the girls would scream. A few windows showed Christmas trees inside and the candles on their branches gave off warm light. Trying to remember a Christmas when her mother was alive, before they came west, she could only dredge up a smile or special dinner but not much after that. How she envied the people inside those houses.

She lit the lamp on the dresser and started to change for dinner. She arranged her hair on top of her head, but then pulled the pins out and let her red locks fall to her shoulders. Her new blouse looked festive, but as she buttoned it up, she wondered where her father was.

After she was dressed, she paced, checking the window, then the door, and the hallway. Where was he?

She was about to give up on Gavin Doyle when a loud knock came at her door.

She ran to open it.

"Bet you were ready to give up on me, weren't you?" Doyle kidded.

"Yes, I was."

Roxy took a few seconds to study her father. She could see the daddy she remembered from years ago. He had a strong profile but seemed smaller than she remembered, since she herself had been much smaller when she last saw him.

"I wondered if you had padding under that Santa suit, she said.

"I may be thicker than you remember, but I can't quite be Santa without some help. "Well, don't just stand there, girl, let's get some grub. I'm starvin'."

Roxy grabbed her coat, slammed the door shut then locked it.

Doyle reached out a large, warm hand to pull her along.

"I have a special place in mind for our Christmas dinner."

"But it's not Christmas yet," Roxy said.

"For me it is. And you're the best present I ever got. Well, besides being born."

He was here, in the flesh, Roxy kept thinking. I'm here with my father, at last.

* * *

They walked two blocks until coming to what looked like a mansion. The large front door had a wreath on it, covered in pine cones and berries. Gavin grabbed the knocker and pounded it against the door.

Instantly a man in a tuxedo answered the knock as if he had been standing there just waiting.

"Ahh, Mr. Doyle, so good to see you again. Your table is ready."

"Thank you, Matthew.

Roxy looked down at her jeans and boots, feeling underdressed.

Making their way across the room, they passed half a dozen tables covered with white cloths, silverware shining in the candlelight from a large chandelier. Two Christmas trees in opposite corners made the room look like the perfect holiday scene.

Her father sat while the maitre d' held Roxy's chair out for her.

"Would the lady care for a glass of wine?"

"This is my daughter, Roxanne. Honey, this is Matthew, owner of the finest restaurant in the whole state."

The man bowed.

"I was not aware you had a daughter, Mr. Doyle."

Sheepishly, Doyle said, "We haven't seen each other in a while."

"Well, now she's here, and it is Christmas time, and you must have some of our special wassail to celebrate. I'll be right back."

After the man was gone, Roxy asked, "So you live here? In Lincoln?"

"No. I come and go. But I stop here a couple times a year. The people are real friendly and—"

"Why didn't you ever contact me?" she demanded. "Do you have any idea what it's been like wondering if I'll ever see you again? You left me alone. I had no family!"

"I wrote you all the time. Didn't you get my letters? And the gifts?" he asked.

"When you first left, I got one letter but never any gifts. The next year I think there was another letter. But that's all."

Doyle reached across the table to stroke her hand.

"After your mother died, the life kind of went out of me. And, I'm ashamed to say it, but every time I looked at you, I saw her." He stared down at the table. "I know you deserved better from me, but I just had to get away. I thought if I could only be by myself and sort things out, I'd come back to you. But I had to make a living to keep sending money for your room and board."

"I never saw a penny. And it won't do any good thinking about getting even. Those people are dead and buried," Roxy said.

"So, there's nothing I can do to make this right?" Doyle's face fell.

"Ahh, here we are," Matthew said, standing there with two crystal glasses on a silver tray. "Some holiday cheer to warm you up."

He gently put a glass in front of each of his guests.

Roxy picked hers up and took a sip of the warm drink.

"That's so good. Reminds me of apple cider, only spicy."

"Exactly right," Matthew said delighted.

"Thank you," Doyle said. "We'll be ready to order in a few minutes. Right now we're doing some catching-up."

"Of course."

Matthew bowed and then walked to another table.

"So how did you ever end up being a bounty hunter?" Roxy asked.

"By accident. I took a job in Denver, as a deputy. When the sheriff was shot dead, I joined the posse to hunt down his killers. Didn't catch 'em, by the way, but that experience gave me a taste of tracking. Surprisingly I had a knack for it. I wandered until one day I saw a wagon train and joined up until we got to Oregon.

"One of the men on the train stole some valuables. Several families pooled their money for a reward. I was full of myself back then and told them all I could get their property back. I found the thief, brought back the goods and got paid. It was all so easy, and I felt valuable again.

"If I knew you were in danger and needed me, I would have come runnin'. You know that, don't you, Roxanne? You've got to know that."

She didn't know that, but he looked so desperate for her forgiveness that she lied. "I know, Daddy."

"Good," Doyle said. "Now let's get us some of that duck they're so famous for here. Does that sound good?"

She nodded.

After giving Matthew their order, Doyle decided it was Roxy's turn to tell him all about herself.

Chapter Nine

She needed another sip of her drink before starting her story.

"I ran away from the beatings and rapes."

It gave her a little pleasure to see her father wince at the thought of his daughter being hurt. But then she told him all about her travels, looking for him. There were many friends she'd made in those years and even a few enemies. But meeting and knowing Clint Adams, the Gunsmith, had been her salvation.

"I met him once," Doyle said. "Fine gentleman. Is that how you got your reputation?"

Roxy nodded. "He took me under his wing and taught me everything I know."

"I bet he did," Doyle said. "He's a legend with the ladies. Did he ever . . .?"

Roxy laughed. "Isn't it a little late for you to talk to me about sex? I'm twenty-four, Dad. I know what's what."

"Of course you do," Doyle said. "I'm sure a beautiful woman such as yourself has to shoo the men away."

"And some I asked to stay," Roxy said, boldly looking her father in the eyes.

Matthew was back leading a waiter pushing a cart to their table.

"Here we are. Two of the chef's finest dinners."

While Matthew pointed and the waiter set the table, Roxy and Doyle saved the rest of their conversation until they were alone.

The duck had been prepared in a thick orange sauce. Roxy had never tasted anything so delicious. It was sweet and crispy at the same time. Doyle ate slowly, enjoying every bite. The small potatoes were roasted in butter and green beans also garnished the plate.

"Didn't I tell you?" Doyle asked. "You'll never get a better meal anywhere. Not in San Francisco or even New York."

"I believe you," Roxy said.

They talked about the food as they ate, avoiding any subject that might spoil the mood. Beneath her happiness, Roxy was feeling some anger at her father for abandoning her. Doyle was swallowing down his guilt along with the duck. But they managed to keep the conversation light.

"Chef Louie has traveled all over the world, bringing recipes back with him," Matthew told them as he served the Boston cream pie. "I hope you enjoy the dessert as much as you did the duck."

"Oh, we will," Roxy said, eager to taste the pie.

"I'll have your waiter bring some coffee." Matthew turned and walked toward the kitchen.

"This has been the best meal of my life," Roxy told her father. "Thank you for giving me this memory."

"I hope to give you a lot more good times, honey."

"I don't know how long I'll be in town," she said. "But now that I've found you, I guess all my plans have changed."

"I never asked why you're in Lincoln to begin with," Doyle said.

"To do a favor for a friend."

Doyle tried giving Matthew some money for their dinner but the man refused, telling him it was a Christmas present and he was glad they had enjoyed it.

They both thanked him for his graciousness and said goodbye, walking out into the cold night.

"Do you have a house here?" Roxy asked as they walked.

"I stay with a lady friend in her house."

Roxy raised her eyebrows. "A lady friend? Are you planning to marry her?"

"Hell no. Your mother was, and will forever be, my only wife. No, Arlene's a widow with no plans to remarry. She understands that I move around a lot and makes no demands on me. How about you? Ever had a husband? Am I a grandfather?"

"No husband, no children," she told him. Changing the subject, she asked if he would like to stop along the way for a drink.

"You might enjoy Big Bertha's," he told her. "We'll have to grab a carriage; it's too far to walk, especially in this snow."

"Let's go."

Roxy didn't want to say goodnight just yet. Her father had promised the town council that he would continue playing the role of Santa Claus for two more days. At least she could count on his staying in town that long. But deep in her heart, she didn't trust him to stay.

* * *

Big Bertha's was a rowdy saloon with a stage in the back. When Roxy and Doyle walked in, a large woman in a tight red satin gown was on that stage, singing loudly. Everyone was in high spirits, laughing and drinking, some singing along.

"Doyle!" a man at the bar shouted.

"Hey, Silas!"

After a few words to his friend, Doyle pushed Roxy toward a corner table, away from most of the noise.

"Do you drink beer?" he asked as they sat down.

"Yes, I do."

"Then sit tight and I'll get us some drinks." Doyle smiled and walked back to the bar.

* * *

"I don't believe it," Vernon said. "It's her again." He pointed toward Roxy Doyle. "Should we leave? What should we do, Stony?"

"Take it easy, fool. Let me think on it a minute," Stony said.

"We could wait outside for Hank," Vernon suggested.

"And just how do we get outta here without her seein' us? No, that would be too obvious."

"Guess we'll have to just sit here, then."

"Guess so," Stony said. "Wait a minute. What have we got to be afraid of? We ain't done nothin' to the precious Lady Gunsmith."

Realizing they hadn't broken any laws in the past few days, Stony sat back in his chair to relax and wait for Hank.

Chapter Ten

"See those two men at that table over there?" Roxy asked Doyle when he returned with their drinks.

"Those two sorry lookin' cowboys?" he asked.

"Yes. Do you know them?"

"I've seen 'em around town, that's about it. Why?"

"They were following me earlier today," she explained. "I finally had to scare them off."

"They're harmless," Doyle said. "Probably all worked up to see a legend up close."

Roxy laughed. "Legend? I don't think so."

"But you will be," he said full of pride. "Why I bet they'll even write them dime novels about my little girl. And with the glory, darlin' daughter, will come the money. You'll be rich."

"Thanks, Dad." She patted his hand.

After taking a big gulp of his beer, Doyle asked, "So, what is this favor you're here to do? You never did tell me."

"I'm here to deliver a necklace to Violet Dunham."

"Violet Dunham . . . Violet Dunham . . ." Doyle rolled the name around in his head a minute. "The cute little girl that belongs to the bakery owner? Ain't the sheriff her stepdaddy?"

"Yes."

"And don't the sheriff hate Mr. Dunham? Seems to me I remember him goin' off on a tirade once about wantin' to kill that man."

"That's why I brought the necklace. It belonged to her grandmother," Roxy said.

"And just how do you propose to get that present to Violet? If Sheriff North knew that necklace was from Dunham, I can't begin to think what he'd do."

Then the idea came to Roxy in a flash.

"What if Santa Claus gave it to Violet and said it was from grandmother, in heaven? The sheriff couldn't be mad about that, could he? And if he came to ask you where you got it, you have time to think up something, leaving Sam out of it. You could do that, couldn't you, Dad?"

"I suppose I could. Maybe tomorrow. The Fair should be in full swing then an . . ."

A tall man with dark eyes and a long dark beard walked through the door and over to the two men Roxy had pointed out. A cold wind followed him into the room.

"Do you know him?" she asked, noticing how her father stared at the newcomer.

"Henry Shepherd. I've crossed his path a couple of times. He's a two-bit horse thief. Spent some time in jail a few years back. Got a wife in Omaha and stays close to home."

"So then why do you look worried?" she asked.

"Somethin' just don't feel right."

* * *

Hank sat with his friends, refusing to turn around and look at Roxy Doyle as his two companions chattered on about her being in town.

"Take it easy. It's just one of them coincidences. They happen all the time. Don't mean a damn thing. But the man she's sittin' with does worry me."

"Why?" Stony asked. "Is he the law?"

"No. Worse. He's a bounty hunter. Thanks to him I spent a year behind bars in Arizona. I'd sure like to get even with that sonofabitch."

"Calm down, Hank," Vernon said. "Remember your plan. No more grabbin' horses, we're here for real money."

"You're right. But now that I see both of 'em over there, I'm thinkin' we need to pull the job tomorrow.

That Christmas party will be crowded all day, it bein' Saturday and all."

"Yeah," Stony agreed. "More people, more confusion. And the bank will be closed early so we can get in with no witnesses. Yeah, now that I think about it, tomorrow's a whole lot better."

* * *

Roxy and Doyle stayed until the music stopped. Bertha walked over to their table, smiling and humming.

"Why, Gavin Doyle! It's been too long, honey. Hope you haven't forgotten about ole Bertha." She stroked his cheek. "And who's this beauty? My replacement?"

"No one could ever replace you, Bertha," Doyle told her. "This is my daughter, Roxanne."

"Glad to meet you," Roxy said. "You have a very . . . unique voice."

"Is that a nice way of saying I sing like shit?"

Roxy laughed. She had never met such a direct woman before.

"Oh no. I meant—"

"It's okay, Miss Doyle. I know I can't sing worth shit. My voice has been shot for years. But this is my place and I'll do whatever the hell I please. Besides, it's my confidence and poise folks come to see. Right, Gavin?"

Doyle nodded. "Sure is."

Bertha waved to the bartender to bring her a drink and squeezed her ample bottom into the chair between Roxy and Doyle.

"So, what occasion has made this father and daughter get-together possible? Christmas? Or did you just miss your dear old daddy?" She looked at Roxy.

"Kind of a reunion," Roxy told her. "We haven't seen each other in years."

"That's a shame," Bertha said. "Family is very important. You'll learn that as you get older. Always make time for your mother and father."

Roxy didn't feel like explaining that her mother had died years ago, and her father abandoned her, so she just nodded.

The bartender walked over with a glass of champagne and set it in front of Bertha then hurried away.

"Now, tell Bertha what your plans are for the rest of the night."

"I guess go home and sleep. It *is* late," Doyle said.

"Late? Why it's still early. Come on, Gavin, don't be an old man."

There had once been something between those two, Roxy could sense it. And Bertha wanted more of whatever they'd had. Should she leave them alone? Or was she reading it all wrong and her father wanted an excuse to leave without hurting the woman's feelings?

"Well, it's been a long day for me. I think I'll find a ride back to my hotel and go to bed," Roxy told Bertha. "Are you staying or leaving, Dad?"

Doyle looked at Bertha and smiled. "I think I'll stay for one more drink. How about we meet around noon in the park tomorrow?"

Roxy stood up. "I'll be there." She walked around to give her father a kiss on the cheek before leaving, and then said, "Goodnight, Bertha."

"Goodnight, young Miss Doyle."

Chapter Eleven

"Are you stayin' the night this time?" Bertha asked Doyle after Roxy left. "Or do you have to make nice with Arlene?"

"Now Bertha, you know damn well I can't stay. But I do have a few hours to spend with you. So instead of throwing one of your tantrums and wastin' time, why don't you go upstairs and get in bed? I'll be up in a few minutes."

"You're a rotten cad," she said. "Did I ever tell you that?"

"Many times."

* * *

Bertha had redone the entire upstairs of her saloon into her private living quarters. There were five large rooms, each furnished with custom-made pieces constructed to her specifications. Her bed had been brought over from France, her lamps came from England, even the wallpaper had been hand-painted in Italy. Bertha had excellent taste and money to waste on whatever she wanted.

Quickly she walked to her bedroom and took a lace nightgown out of the closet, got into bed and waited for Gavin Doyle to come to her. Each time they made love she hoped he'd see how ordinary Arlene was and choose Bertha. But each time he went home to his dull girl-friend.

When she heard the sound of his shoes on the stairs, she got excited and could feel her sheet getting wet beneath her.

* * *

Even before Doyle walked into Bertha's bedroom, he started to get hard. Something about that woman drove him senseless.

By the time he opened her door, he had his trousers unbuttoned, his shirt in his hands and almost fell trying to kick his boots off.

"What took you so long?" Bertha demanded.

"I wanted to finish my beer. I plan to work up a big thirst in that grand bed of yours. And it was only ten minutes."

Tossing the rest of his clothes in a pile, Doyle climbed into bed and on top of Bertha. He sunk into her, almost as if she were one big pillow. Her scent always drove him wild and tonight she tasted like she'd doused herself in vanilla. He buried his face in her soft, smooth breasts, kissing her hard nipples. He had to restrain himself from biting too hard as she moaned with pleasure.

"Get down there, honey. You know what I like."

Pushing himself down her body, he rested his head between her legs and licked at the wetness between her thighs.

"You are the sweetest tasting woman," he managed to say. "I want to eat you up."

"Be my guest."

They stayed like that for a while, all the time both of them trying hard to hold back their release.

Without warning, Bertha flipped him over on his back and crawled on her knees to take his cock into her mouth. Garvin Doyle was all man and for an hour or two he was her man. She sucked him while rubbing his balls with the palm of one hand. With the other she moved up and down the shaft of his large penis.

He'd once told her that no other woman would do the things she'd do in bed. Then why didn't he want to be with her every night, she wondered as she enjoyed the sound of his heavy breathing.

They knew each other well enough to pace themselves and rolled on their backs to relax a moment. She ran her nails through the hair on his chest while he nuzzled her neck.

They started kissing until he couldn't resist any longer and got on top of her to push his penis deep inside her. The sudden movement took her breath away and she almost passed out from the excitement of him.

The first thrust felt so good that Doyle stayed there a minute. But when he opened his eyes and saw her pleasure, he started pushing in and out of her. Slowly at first, but soon they were moving so quickly the bed shook beneath them.

They tried making it last longer without success. Before they knew it, Bertha was screaming her climax and Doyle was shouting his.

* * *

"Did you hear that?" a man at the bar downstairs asked. "Sounded like someone's gettin' hurt."

"More like gettin' fucked," the bartender said and laughed.

Chapter Twelve

Roxy had the driver leave her off down by the stable to check on her horse. If she was going to be in town longer, there were arrangements to be made for the animal's care.

As she approached the side door, it opened and the light from inside blinded her a moment.

"Why, Miss Doyle! I been wonderin' about you. Last night your plan was to stay in town two days. Is that still true?"

"No, Woody. I'm not sure, but I think a few more days."

"Well, I'll take care of Nona for as long as you want. She's sure a friendly animal. The other horses like havin' her around."

"Nona?" Roxy asked. "Are you talking about my horse? The Morgan?"

"Sure, Miss Doyle. Remember when I asked you what her name was? You told me Nona."

Roxy laughed. "I think I told you 'No Name' but I'll keep Nona. It seems to suit her."

"Good," Woody said.

"Before I go I'd like to see Nona," Roxy said. All of a sudden she was having feelings for the horse. Maybe it was because of her having a name.

Woody walked her back to the stall and the Morgan came closer to see Roxy. They visited for a few moments until Nona got bored and turned away.

"I'm staying at the Baron House. You were right; it's a beautiful place. Do you need any money now or can we settle up when I leave?"

"I'll keep track of your bill. Don't need nothin' now."

"Thank you so much."

The two of them were outside the stable when Roxy remembered a message she wanted to send.

"Can you tell me where the closest telegraph office is?"

"Right next to your hotel, Miss Doyle. Guess you just didn't notice it," Woody said.

"You've been such a help," Roxy said. "Hope you and your family have a Merry Christmas."

"Same to you, Miss."

As she walked back toward her hotel, Roxy realized how tired she was. The inside of the telegraph office was dark. Her telegram to Sam would have to wait until morning.

* * *

The snow had continued throughout the night. After a breakfast of eggs and bacon, Roxy walked next door to the telegraph office.

"Really coming down out there," the key operator said.

Roxy brushed off her coat. "Must be four inches deep."

"At least," the young man agreed. "Can I help you?"

"I hope you're getting extra pay having to work on Christmas."

"Workin' on holidays is just part of the job, Miss."

"Well, Merry Christmas, anyway," Roxy said.

"And to you also," he said. "Now, what can I do for you?"

"I'd like to send a message to Omaha, to a Mr. Samuel Dunham. I have his address here." Roxy took a small piece of paper out of her pocket.

"No problem, Miss." The man began typing in the name and address of the recipient and then looked up. "And the message you want to send?"

Roxy looked around the small room. She had been the only person there, aside from the operator, but she still was cautious of a stranger overhearing what she wanted to tell Sam. Leaning forward she relayed her message in a low voice.

After a few taps of the keys, the message was ready.

"Anything to add?" the man asked. "Is that all?"

Roxy nodded.

"And do you want to come back for an answer, or should I bring it to you?"

"About how long do you think it'll take?"

"Oh, a few hours I suppose. Especially if he's expecting to hear from you. Is he?"

"Yes. I told him I'd stay in touch."

"I go for lunch at noon but other than that, I'll be here til six."

"Thanks," Roxy said. "I'll be back."

Before going outside, Roxy took a pair of wool gloves out of the drawstring purse hanging from her wrist. Pulling the collar of her heavy coat up toward her ears, she walked out into the blustery morning.

* * *

After making sure The Lady Gunsmith was too far away to notice him, Henry Shepherd rushed into the telegraph office, slamming the door behind him. Then he stomped his boots leaving a trail of wet snow.

"That wind is enough to frostbite a man," he said to the key operator, shaking flakes off his sleeves.

"Sure is."

"Come on now, Arnett, ain't you got a friendly word for me?"

The man looked at Hank like he had just had a dose of castor oil. "We ain't exactly what you'd call friends, are we now?"

"Maybe not," Shepherd grudgingly agreed. "More like employer and peon seein' as how I've paid you to do some odd jobs for me over the years."

Arnett grunted. "So tell me what brings you here today so I can get on with my business."

"It's your business I'm here about."

"What do you mean?" Arnett asked.

"Just what did Lady Gunsmith want? Was she here to send a telegram?"

"You know I can't talk about my customers."

Those dark eyes of Shepherd's glared into Arnett Long's pale blue ones. "That's never stopped you before."

"Well, you paid me them other times."

"I told you the money will come when the job's over."

Arnett grunted. Before he could back away, Shepherd grabbed the front of his shirt, pulling him over the counter, close enough that the clerk could feel the furious man's breath on his face.

"Now are you gonna tell me what the bitch wanted, or do I have to break a few of your fingers so you can't do your job no longer?"

Arnett pulled away, and after smoothing down the front of his shirt, said, "She wanted to send a telegram. Why else would she come here?"

"Just tell me what the hell the telegram said," Shepherd demanded.

Looking at the angry man standing in front of him, Arnett knew Shepherd could easily beat the tar out of him. Or get his gang to just kill him. But he'd been born with a bad temper and hated having anyone push him around. He also knew lying to Shepherd would only buy him a little time. The big man was all muscle and very little brains. He couldn't even read the telegram if Arnett handed it to him. But what was the point? And the money was always needed.

"She sent it to someone in Omaha. Said she…"

"Man or woman?"

"What?"

"Did she send it to a man or a woman?"

"A man."

Shepherd nodded.

"Said she'd be stayin' here, in town, a few more days because she had found her father."

"Huh," Shepherd thought a moment. "And just who's her father?"

"How the hell should I know. I don't question my customers. I just take their words and . . ."

"You better watch that mouth of yours, son. It's gonna get you in a whole lot of trouble."

It was Shepherd's eyes that scared Arnett the most.

"Alls I'm sayin' is I don't know who her father is. But if her last name is Doyle, I'd guess her father's named Doyle unless she's married or somethin'."

Suddenly Shepherd remembered who the man in Big Bertha's was. Gavin Doyle, the bounty hunter who had chased him across two states. And the reason he had put in time at that prison in Arizona.

"And somethin' about gettin' a Christmas present . . ." Arnett started. But Shepherd hurried out of the office.

Chapter Thirteen

The big clock on City Hall chimed twelve as Roxy made her way through the snow. She could see the festivities had already begun in the square. But there wasn't any sign of Santa Claus. Her heart sank at the thought that she would never see her father . . . again.

Children chased each other, shouting and laughing. More booths were set up than had been there yesterday. Roxy strolled over to get a cup of cocoa. Between the children filled with excitement, the adults hawking their holiday goods and music coming from a nearby gazebo, it was almost impossible to carry on a decent conversation when Julie Dunham waved Roxy over.

As Julie talked, Roxy nodded, only able to hear a few words here and there. But all the while she was wondering if she should tell the woman about the Christmas present beforehand? Maybe if she was prepared, understood why Sam wanted his daughter to have the necklace, she'd be understanding. Would it make Julie angry or should Roxy stick with her plan to have Santa give the necklace to the child?

Finally, there was a moment of quiet and Roxy asked, "Is Violet here today?"

"Oh, that child was up all night. She's so excited to see what Santa will bring her."

"What does she want this year?" Roxy asked.

"A doll, a new dress . . . you know, what every little girl wants."

Roxy remembered the Christmas presents she had wished for when she was ten but never received.

Abruptly a loud squeal erupted from a crowd of youngsters as a sleigh pulled by two horses glided to a stop in front of them.

"Santa! Santa Claus!"

Roxy's heart felt as if it was swelling with love for the man in the red suit. Quickly she said goodbye to Julie and ran over to see her father.

"And have you been good this year?" Doyle was asking a small boy. When the child nodded, Doyle asked, "Every day of the year? All year long?"

The boy's face drooped, and he looked as if he would start bawling.

"Well, most every day?" Doyle tried to give the kid an out.

"Almost every day," he said proudly. " 'Cept for the time I hit Billy Hobson."

A smaller girl stepped forward. "It wasn't his fault, Santa. Everybody wants to hit Billy."

Doyle tried not to laugh. "Are you his sister?"

The girl nodded.

"You're a good sister, defending your brother." Turning toward the boy he said, "I'll overlook your temper this time, but promise it won't happen again?"

"Swear to God. An' if it does, my Pa said he'll take a switch to my bottom."

"Well, that's good enough for me." Doyle smiled a big one for the boy.

Roxy saw her chance to talk with her father for a moment and walked up.

"Okay, kids, let ole Santa get situated over on that bench and we'll see if there's some presents in his bag."

Without a second of hesitation, the children ran to the bench he had pointed out.

Roxy hugged Doyle, into a tight squeeze.

"Afraid I wouldn't show up, weren't you, honey?" he asked.

"No," she said releasing him from her arms. "I was just . . ."

"I'm never leavin' you again, Roxy. You'll always know where I am if I'm not nearby."

Roxy hated to cry, thought it was a sign of weakness, but she couldn't help herself and let a few tears run down her cheeks.

"Better stop that or your face'll freeze," he said.

She laughed.

"Do you still want me to give the little Dunham girl that necklace? Cause if you do, the time is now. You never told me if the necklace was valuable, but I been thinkin' we can tell anyone who asks that it's just a bauble. Don't wanna get people riled up about it. Know what I mean?"

For the time being Roxy thought it best to lie. "It's just colored glass and gold paint."

"Okay, so where is it?"

"Back in my hotel room," Roxy said. "I'll go get it."

"I'll try to control these little savages until you come back. Maybe leave Violet til last so as not to draw attention to her."

"Good idea."

Roxy hurried across the slippery road toward her hotel. In spite of the cold, the day had turned out sunny, reflecting the white of the snow, causing her to squint as she walked.

Inside the hotel she was greeted with a loud, Merry Christmas, from Mr. Clark, who stood behind the desk.

She smiled but never slowed her step heading for the stairs.

Reaching her room, her happiness suddenly turned to caution when she noticed the door slightly ajar. She drew her gun and slowly peeked inside.

Seeing her clothes scattered across the floor she shouted, "Come out of there! Now!"

When no one showed themselves, Roxy slowly walked into the room.

Chairs were in pieces, a lamp was broken, lying in a puddle of oil. The pitcher and basin on the table had been smashed. Then like a bolt of lightning it struck her, and she ran through the sitting room to the bedroom.

The painting over the bed had been tossed across the room. She ran to it and inspected the back of the frame. The necklace was gone.

"Oh no, no, no," she repeated to herself.

Would her father think she had grown into a stupid woman? After he had gone on about her becoming a legend, could she stand to see the disappointment in his eyes? She sat on the edge of the bed and tried to calm herself. And what would she tell Sam?

After five minutes of feeling sorry for herself, she got angry, straightened up and stormed back down to the lobby.

Roger Clark knew there was something very wrong when he saw Roxy Doyle marching toward him.

"Why, Miss Doyle, are you alright? You look . . . so . . . upset."

"Do I?" she asked, trying not to shout at the man. "My room has been ransacked. Some property was stolen that has special sentimental value to me. So please, Mr. Clark, tell me you didn't let anyone into my room."

"Of course not. You're the only guest registered to that room and you're the only person we would allow inside."

"Except for the chambermaid, I assume. Or any other hotel employees. Am I right?"

"Well, yes," he said sheepishly. "But I can assure you we check out all our people very thoroughly before we hire."

"I'm going to sit on that divan over there while you go for the law."

"Of course, Miss Doyle. Right away. Just let me get my wife to man the desk."

Chapter Fourteen

It was finally Violet Dunham's turn to talk to Santa. It had taken all her patience being at the end of the line, and it was so cold, but she was on her best behavior.

Santa lifted the little girl and sat her on his lap.

"And you wouldn't be Violet, would you?"

Her eyes seemed close to popping right out of her head.

"How did you know?" she asked in a soft whisper.

The man laughed. "Santa knows all the children in all the towns."

She sat there speechless.

"So tell me, Violet, what do you want for Christmas?"

"I want my mama to let daddy come back home so we can all live together in the same house."

Doyle felt as if he was somehow looking at his own little girl. How many nights must Roxy have wished he'd come home? She was so young when her Ma died. And he'd just gone off and left her.

Trying to cheer the girl up, he said, "Well, honey, I don't think your father will fit in my sack. But I can pass on your wish, and while you're waiting, how about a doll?"

When he pulled the gift that had been donated by the women's league, out of his burlap bag, Violet smiled and grabbed the ragdoll, hugging it to her heart.

"Thank you, Santa. I love her."

"Well, you've been a very good girl this year." He patted Violet's cheek before standing her back on the ground.

After making sure that all the children were happy, Doyle looked around for Roxy. While wondering what to do next, several women approached him with hot cider and cookies.

Enjoying a break, he checked the big clock and decided to give his daughter another hour before going to look for her.

* * *

"And how long were you gone, Miss Doyle?" the sheriff asked.

"Maybe two hours. No more," Roxy said.

"And you didn't see anyone suspicious this morning? Or maybe last night?"

"Well, there were these men in Big Bertha's. I'd had trouble with two of them yesterday."

"What kind of trouble?"

"They were following me in town, but I set 'em straight," Roxy said.

"Probably just curious to see Lady Gunsmith. I bet you have admirers in every county."

"Those men weren't admirers, Sheriff. They were trouble; I could smell it on 'em. And I saw them again at Big Bertha's. They were joined by a tall man with the darkest eyes. I think his name was Hank."

"That wouldn't be Hank Shepherd would it?" Sheriff North asked.

Roxy shrugged. "I don't know."

"Well, Miss Doyle, I'll have my deputy look over your room. Was anything valuable taken?"

"A necklace," Roxy told the lawman. "It was a family heirloom, not worth much but I'd really like to have it back. It's very important to me."

She looked up at him and smiled a weak helpless woman smile that no man could resist. It always worked. Most men were helpless and stupid when it came to women.

"I'm sure Mr. Clark here can have someone go clean up your room so you can get to sleep soundly tonight," The sheriff told her. "That is unless you're too upset to be by yourself?"

"Thank you," Roxy said thinking that it was the thief who should be upset when she found out where he was hiding. "I'll be fine."

Roger Clark smiled and patted Roxy's shoulder.

"Don't you worry, Miss Doyle, I'll have Harry go upstairs immediately and tidy up. And if there's anything else you need, day or night, please don't hesitate to call on me or my wife."

Before she could thank the sheriff and Mr. Clark, Gavin Doyle came racing into the lobby of The Baron House Hotel. When he saw Roxy, he hurried over to her.

"Roxy, honey, are you okay?" Then he recognized Sheriff North. "Lloyd, what are you doing here? Is something wrong?"

"Calm down now, Doyle, no one's hurt. There was just a little . . ."

"Someone broke into my room and stole the necklace I told you about, Dad."

"Dad?" North said, surprised. "You two are related? Well, it does make sense. Roxy Doyle, the Lady Gunsmith and Gavin Doyle, the bounty hunter. What a team."

Chapter Fifteen

"What makes Hank think the bank will be empty?" Vernon asked.

"It's Christmas," Stony said. "He says the bank's always closed on Christmas Day."

They made their way along the empty streets toward the bank. When they got close, Stony stopped walking and snapped at Vernon, "Not the front, fool! Follow me."

He led Vernon around to the back of the bank and stopped at the rear door.

"What now?" Vernon asked.

"Just keep watch," Stony said. "I'll get the door open."

"But it's locked," Vernon whispered.

"That's why I'm here," Stony said. "And stop whisperin'. We're all alone."

Vernon kept his eyes open nervously while Stony worked on the locked door. Before long he heard the latch click and the door open.

"Let's go," Stony said.

He entered, then Vernon followed nervously. As soon as they were inside, they became aware that someone else was there, as well.

"Somebody's here," Vernon said.

"Now you can whisper," Stony told him, drawing his gun. "Come on."

They moved from the back of the bank toward the front and saw a man standing at the open safe door. The man, a tall, slender middle-aged fellow, saw them at the same time.

"What are you doin' here?" he demanded. "The bank's closed."

"So whatayou doin' here?" Stony asked.

"I'm the bank manager."

"Well, that's good," Stony said, "because we're bank robbers."

"What?" The manager put his hand on the safe door, as if to slam it shut.

"Don't do it!" Stony said, sticking his gun in the man's ribs. "You're a dead man if you close that safe. That's good. Now move away from it . . . further . . . that's it. Vernon, get the money."

That was when Vernon knew Stony intended to kill the man, anyway. Otherwise, he wouldn't have said his name."

Vernon found a bank bag and began filling it with the money. He needed a second one, as well.

"Is there any more money here?" Stony asked the manager.

"No," the man said. "I just finished putting it all in the safe."

"Did you count it?"

"I did."

"How much is there?" Stony asked.

"Over fifty thousand dollars."

"I thought there'd be more," Stony said.

"There's more than one in town here," the manager said.

"That's okay," Stony said. "We're only robbin' this one."

"Are you finished?" the manager asked.

"Not quite." Stony pointed his gun at the man's stomach and pulled the trigger. As the man clutched his belly and fell, Stony said, "Now, we're done."

"What the heck did ya do that for?" Vernon demanded. "We got the money."

"We don't want him raisin' the alarm," Stony explained. "Now let's get our horses and get outta town!"

* * *

"Sheriff North! I been lookin' everywhere for you," a young man with a deputy badge pinned to his heavy coat ran to the sheriff's side. "You gotta come right away."

"Calm down, Kilborn, you're gettin' yourself all riled up."

"But Sheriff, the bank's been robbed. In the middle of the day! The bank Manager, Mister Stern, was shot . . ."

"Is he dead?" North asked.

" 'fraid so," the deputy said trying to catch his breath.

"Aww, shit," North groaned. "What the hell was Cal doin' there on Christmas Day?"

"You want me to go fetch his wife?" Kilborn asked.

"No. You go to the bank. Ask around and see if anybody saw something or heard anything . . ."

"I'm on my way," Kilborn said as he ran back into the cold.

Realizing that Doyle and Roxy were still nearby, North turned toward them.

"I've known Cal for twenty years, maybe more. I should be the one to go tell Irene the bad news."

Doyle tossed his red hat on a chair and started to un-button his Santa costume. "I'm goin' with you, Lloyd. Cal was always decent to me; I owe him this much."

Roxy decided she could use her time better looking for the men who stole Violet's necklace.

Chapter Sixteen

As soon as Roxy Doyle walked into the street, Arnett Long came running out of the telegraph office waving a piece of paper.

"Miss Doyle! Your telegram!"

She had almost forgotten about her message to Sam.

"You didn't have to come looking for me," Roxy said. "With everything that's been going on today, I guess I forgot all about it."

"Come inside where it's warm." He pointed to his office. "I have coffee made if you'd like some."

"Thanks," Roxy said, "coffee sounds real good."

"It's pretty quiet in there this time of year," he said as they walked. "But after the holidays when everyone sends out thank-yous for their presents, I'm hoppin' around like a mad rabbit."

He held the door open for her and ushered her to a chair. Then he handed her the telegram.

"You can read this while I get a clean cup.

As the man walked away, Roxy held the telegram up to the sunlight that was streaming through the window.

It was from Sam: MISS YOU, TOO, SWEETHEART. THANKS AGAIN. HURRY HOME.

Strange, she thought and read the 8 words again. Sam had never called her sweetheart. No mention of Christmas. And no name at the bottom.

"Here we go," Arnett said, handing Roxy a cup of coffee. "If you want milk or . . ."

"This is fine," Roxy said. "Don't trouble yourself."

Arnett settled down in the chair next to Roxy. A little too close, she thought, but didn't say anything.

"So," the man started, "you sounded upset about what's been going on today."

She nodded.

"I'm a real good listener, if you feel like unloadin'. Did you know Mr. Stern?"

"Awful news about him."

"Yes, it is. And my hotel room was ransacked."

"Was any money stolen?" he asked too eagerly for her taste.

"I would never leave money behind in my room. Never."

"So just some stuff busted up?" he asked. "I'm sure the hotel can replace the furniture or whatever."

"I suppose."

"As long as nothin' valuable was taken, it really don't matter, does it?"

"I guess not."

Roxy wondered if Arnett Long was just one of those long-winded men she'd run into or if he was nervous about something. When he offered her a second cup of coffee she decided to find out.

As he walked over to the potbelly stove, she studied the small room. Then she studied him.

"I bet you're a real popular guy here in town," she said, as he poured.

"Why do you say that?" he asked.

"Well, everyone who comes in here has news or is waiting for news. You know all the goings-on, everybody's business."

His eyebrows jumped a little.

"Now. Miss Doyle, you must know that we operators have an ethical code. We're held to very high standards on account of the fact that we deal with the public. And most times we have to deliver bad news. Especially in times of war . . ."

"Or out here where the law can be a bit . . . sketchy and awful things happen."

Arnett nodded.

"Or," Roxy continued, "when you're strong-armed by an unscrupulous person to pass along the contents of someone else's messages. I bet that's happened to you a time or two."

"Oh, you wouldn't believe the scum I've come across. There was this one time . . ." Arnett caught himself just as an older gentleman walked through the door.

"Can you help me send a telegram?" the man asked.

Arnett smiled at Roxy, looking relieved. " 'Scuse me."

As Arnett helped his customer, Roxy finished her coffee. Setting the cup down, she stood and waved good-bye to the operator.

"Merry Christmas, Miss Doyle," Arnett called after her.

"Same to you," Mr. Long.

* * *

Doyle stood by helplessly as Sheriff North tried to calm Irene Stern.

"I told that man not to go to the bank today. But it was like his second home." She sobbed into North's shirt. "You know how stubborn he was, Lloyd."

"Yes, I do, Irene."

Doyle wondered if it would be bad manners to sit down or should he remain standing? He shifted from foot to foot. Even though he had witnessed similar scenes play out in different towns with different widows and children, it was always hard to watch.

When Irene's knees started to buckle and her hysterics grew, Lloyd looked to Doyle for help guiding the widow into a chair.

Sitting down only seemed to make things worse. She started to scream and wail, which surprised Lloyd since he'd never heard one kind word pass between the couple.

"Can I get you some water?" Doyle offered.

"Who the hell are you," Irene growled. "Lloyd, why did you bring some stranger into my house? Too afraid to deliver bad news by yourself?"

The sheriff looked helplessly at Doyle.

"Irene, this is Gavin Doyle, this year's Santa Claus. He was an acquaintance of Cal's. He thought he might be of some comfort."

"I'm sorry," Irene said meekly. "I just never had my husband killed before. I'm not sure how to act."

"Mr. Doyle here is a famous bounty hunter," Lloyd told her. "Maybe you heard of him?"

"No."

"Well, we're lucky to have him in town. He might be of some help finding the men who shot Cal."

Doyle hadn't planned to stay in town past New Years Day. He'd been working on a few tips he'd gotten about some wanted men riding through Colorado. But now that he had Roxy back in his life, who knew what he'd be doing next month.

"I want those bastards to pay," Irene said. "And, Mr. Doyle, if you make some extra money along the way, all the better."

Chapter Seventeen

The only thing Roxy could think to do was head back to her hotel. All festivities in the park had abruptly stopped when the bank had been robbed. Mothers rushed their children home to spend a safe day away from Main Street. While booths were still standing, banners had been ripped from their poles and now laid soggy in the snow. The sun hid behind a dark cloud and the gay atmosphere that had existed only an hour before had transformed into one of gloom.

"Hey, Miss Doyle," Harry, the bellman, called as Roxy came through the front door.

"Hey, Harry," she called back.

"Quite a day, huh?"

"Sure is."

"Guess you heard about poor Mr. Stern?"

"I did."

"What a shame," Harry said. "The man was a saint. But that wife of his…" he shook his head. "None of us knew how he lasted twenty-one years with that shrew."

"I guess love is truly blind," Roxy said.

"Amen."

"Is everything closed up today?" Roxy asked, realizing how hungry she was.

"You mean like cafes an' such?"

Roxy nodded.

"Sorry, yes. But the Clarks serve a nice dinner on holidays. I can go tell them to set another place?"

"If it wouldn't be any trouble. I could even take a plate up to my room so as not to spoil . . ."

"That would never do. I know they'd love to have a famous person such as yourself at their table. Your presence will make the holiday even more special."

Roxy never thought of herself as famous. In fact, every time someone recognized her or made a fuss, she felt somewhat embarrassed. But before she could say another word, Harry was halfway across the room, heading for a door marked: PRIVATE.

She could hear voices coming from behind the door where she suspected the family lived. Wanting to go upstairs to her room to clean up a little, she stood there unsure of what to do next. Her indecision lasted only a moment when a middle-aged woman opened the door and started toward Roxy with a big smile.

"Miss Doyle, I'm Matilda Clark; my husband, Roger, and I own the hotel. Harry told me that you'll be all alone on Christmas?"

"Well . . ."

"No, no, we can't have that. Please, join us for dinner. We always have so much food. Be prepared is my motto." As the woman spoke, she wiped her hand on a gingham apron around her waist.

"This is so generous of you, Mrs. Clark . . ."

"Matilda. We don't stand on formality here."

"Then please call me, Roxy."

Matilda nodded. "Good, now we're friends. I hope you're hungry."

"I feel like I haven't eaten for days," Roxy said.

"Do you want to go to your room first? Maybe drop off your coat?" Before Roxy could say a word, Matilda added, "Our chambermaids cleaned up your room while you were out."

When Matilda took a breath, Roxy told her, "Yes, I would like to wash up and change."

"Fine. While you do that, I'll finish up in the kitchen. When you're ready, just come on in. Our dining room is right behind that door marked Private."

Roxy nodded and hurried up the stairs. "Thanks again," she called over her shoulder.

Even though she knew she'd find her room in order, her heart started to race before putting the key in the lock. Hesitating a moment, she reached for her gun and held it in her other hand for extra security. Then she slowly walked into her room.

* * *

Everything was not only in its place but cleaned and shined. The painting that had hung over the bed was back on the wall. She couldn't help herself and lifted it to have a look again for the necklace, hoping that somehow it was there. But it was still gone.

Satisfied that she was safe, Roxy tossed her coat on the bed, went to the dresser where she had laid out her toiletries, and brushed her long red hair. Before changing into a clean blouse, she washed her face and hands. The turquoise necklace that had been her mother's never left her person. Sometimes it adorned her hat, other times she wore it as a necklace. To commemorate her first Christmas with her father in years, she strung the large stone around her neck. Finally she was ready to join the Clarks downstairs.

The lobby was quiet; Harry was not at his station. When she passed the front desk, she noticed a sign wishing guests a Merry Christmas and instructing anyone needing to see the management to come back in two hours.

As Roxy walked across the thick carpet to the dining room door, she again enjoyed the decorations and the beautiful pine tree covered with candles and glass ornaments. A fire was roaring in the large fireplace, everything was almost perfect. If only her father was there.

Where was he?

Matilda opened the door and wonderful aromas drifted past her, welcoming Roxy into the room.

"The guest of honor's here!" Harry shouted as he put a large bowl of mashed potatoes on the long table.

Roger Clark seemed to be supervising the activities while several people Roxy had yet to meet, scurried in and out of the kitchen.

"Miss Doyle, so very glad you decided to join us. Christmas is no day to spend alone. Come, sit." He guided her to a chair. "Now, would you prefer port, or we have some mulled wine in that punchbowl over there," he pointed to a round table in the corner.

"Mulled wine?" Roxy asked.

"Oh, you must try it," Clark went on. "My wife is from Kent—that's in England. This recipe has been handed down through her family for generations."

Roxy smiled. "Thank you."

When the man put the silver cup in her hand, she was surprised it was warm. There were cloves and other spices floating on the top of the red beverage. As she brought it to her lips, the fragrance of apples and oranges comforted her.

Chapter Eighteen

The youngest member of the Clark family was Edwin, but everyone called him Eddy.

"Our other two are all grown up and many miles away. Hopefully we'll get together in the Spring for Easter," Matilda said as she passed a platter of spiced roast beef.

There were eight of them seated at the table. Besides the Clark family, Harry and Roxy, three guests—a young couple and an elderly man on his way to Iowa—were all sharing stories of past Christmases. The table was covered with so many plates and bowls that just the sight of it was overwhelming. Every once in a while, the air erupted with laughter and gay conversation. Roxy didn't want to spoil the evening but had no nostalgic memories to speak of. Luckily, she was saved by the curious questions of ten-year-old Eddy.

The boy picked at his dinner, kicked his feet restlessly under the table waiting for the adults to finish their boring chatter. When he could contain himself no longer, he blurted, "Miss Doyle, is it true you know Belle Starr? And the James Gang?"

The room seemed suddenly sucked of the joy while everyone waited for Roxy to answer.

"Well, Eddy," she started, looking down at the boy's anxious smile, "yes. I've run across a lot of bad people in my life."

"Were you afraid?" he asked.

"I sure was."

"An' do you think it was maybe one of those bad people that broke up your room?"

It was obvious from the other diners' expressions that they hadn't heard about Roxy's trouble.

"Someone broke into your room, Miss Doyle?" the elderly man asked. Then he looked at his hosts. "Mr. Clark, I was led to believe this was a respectable, safe hotel. Was I incorrect?"

"No, no, Mr. Hood," Roger Clark told the man. "I can assure you this has never happened before. But the holidays always bring so many strangers to town. I promise, you are very safe here."

The young couple seemed unconcerned and kept eating. But Mr. Hood frowned, pushing his plate away.

Eddy was undaunted and kept rattling on about how he wanted to go out West and be a gunfighter.

Roxy put down her fork and reached out to pat the boy's hand.

"Why would you ever want to leave this beautiful house? And your parents? You would give up your room to sleep on the ground, jumping at every move in the brush?

You would trade your mother's cooking for a diet of beans and jerky? Would you leave behind friends and family to be hated by strangers?"

Matilda smiled her thanks to Roxy as she watched her son's expression change.

Mr. Clark stood up and clapped his hands, snapping everyone's attention back to the feast they were enjoying.

"Is everyone ready for dessert? Matilda has been baking for days."

"Mr. Hood, if I remember correctly, you expressed a fondness for pumpkin pie?"

That brought a slight smile to the old man's face.

"I think I can manage a slice," he grumbled.

"And coming from England, my wife has brought her family's recipe for mince pies."

As Matilda was on her way to the kitchen to bring out coffee, a loud knock suddenly shook the door.

"Roxanne! Are you there, girl?"

"Dad?" she called back.

Roger Clark got up to open the door and was stunned to see Santa Claus standing before him.

Gavin Doyle extended his hand. "Mr. Clark, I hope I'm not interrupting your Christmas dinner, but I'm here to see my daughter."

"Right this way." Clark ushered Doyle into the room. "Won't you have a seat? We're just about to have some dessert. Would you care for a piece of pie? Coffee?"

"Coffee would be fine." Doyle pulled a chair over next to Roxy.

Eddy sat wide-eyed.

"You know Santa?" he asked Roxy.

"Very well," she laughed.

* * *

After coffee, Roxy and Doyle went up to her room to have a quiet conversation.

"How's Mrs. Stern?" Roxy asked.

"Not exactly how you'd expect."

"I heard their marriage was a little . . . bumpy," Roxy said.

"More than a little. That woman must be part crocodile from the amount of tears she shed."

"You don't think she had anything to do with the robbery?" Roxy asked.

"No. It was just a horrible tragedy," Doyle said. "Seems bad things happen around the holidays. Did you ever notice that?"

Roxy thought a moment. "Can't say I have."

A fire was blazing in the sitting room, and before he sat down in front of it, Doyle removed his red coat, hat, and mittens.

"Whew, that's better. Any word about your necklace?"

Roxy pulled a chair up beside him. "No, and I feel like I failed Sam."

"Have you heard from him?"

"He answered my telegram, but it just . . . didn't sound like him. Nothing specific, but it felt strange."

"Other than that," Doyle asked, "you're okay?"

"Since I found you, I'm good."

"Well, I came to tell you something, Roxy, girl."

She looked up at him. "What?"

"The sheriff's puttin' together a posse. I had a tough time talking him out of riding after those crooks today. That fool would have run straight into a blizzard. But if I'm reading the signs right, tomorrow will be better."

"And you came to tell me, you're going with them. Right?"

"Now don't worry, honey . . ."

"I'm not going to worry, because I'm going with you."

Gavin had to laugh. "You always were a bullheaded girl. But I have to forbid you to come."

Now it was Roxy who laughed.

"Forbid me? I'm a grown woman, Dad. I'll go and do whatever I please.

"But Roxy . . ."

"No more forbidding nonsense. What time do we leave tomorrow?"

Chapter Nineteen

Roxy arranged for the Clarks to hold her room while she was gone. Matilda made breakfast for them before they went to the stable to get their horses. When they rode up to the front of the sheriff's office they saw a group of men.

"What's this?" Sheriff North asked, looking at Roxy mounted on her horse. "Doyle, I can't take responsibility for a woman on the trail. It's too dangerous out there. And these are killers we're goin' after."

"Apparently you're not familiar with my daughter's reputation, Sheriff."

"I can handle myself," she told the lawman.

North threw up his hands. "Fine, I haven't got time to argue."

As the posse rode out of Lincoln, the sun shone brightly. Icicles hanging from buildings along Main Street dripped as they warmed. Doyle knew that tracks covered by snow last night and impossible to see, would now be melting down to the black dirt beneath. And the burned-out remnants of a campfire from the previous night and this morning would be guiding the posse in the right direction.

"I've heard tales about how Clint Adams always hunts down the bad guys even if he's not involved with the crime," Doyle said to Roxy as they rode next to each other. "I call that misguided. What do you call it?"

Roxy knew what her father was getting at. He was trying to show her the importance of staying on target and not letting personal matters fog her thinking.

"Well, I'm not Clint so there's no need to worry," she said.

"I'm not so sure," Doyle told her. "What about that necklace that got stolen? This Dunham fella coulda been settin' you up. Did you ever think about that?"

"Sure, I've thought about that," she admitted. "That's why I have to find it."

"And if it turns out your 'friend' hasn't been too friendly to you, what then?"

"I'll call in the law . . . after I beat the tar outta him."

"Well, daughter, if you need help showin' this man the error of his ways, count me in."

"But I never know where you are or how to get a hold of you, Dad."

"That's all gonna change. You have my word on it."

The two had lagged behind while they talked and now heard the sheriff shouting from the front of the pack.

"They was here!" North pointed and jumped off his horse.

Two of the riders joined him around a pile of black ashes. Together the three men sifted through the remnants with their boots.

"Look Sheriff, one of them bank bands they use to wrap the money with."

Sheriff North picked up the partially burnt piece of red paper.

"They probably split up the cash. And from the looks of all the tracks in every direction, they went their separate ways."

Garvin Doyle carefully dismounted and inspected the scene. "I'd say there are three of 'em."

A short man who wore a coon-skin hat nodded. "He's right."

"Well, with seven of us, and three of them we can afford to send two men after each robber. That leaves someone who can go back to town."

All the men looked at Roxy.

"I'm staying with my father," Roxy told them.

She was well aware that she sounded like a frightened woman who needed her parent, which certainly wasn't the case. The truth was, she was afraid to let him out of her sight.

"You heard the lady," Doyle said. "The two of us will take those tracks headin' east."

A heavyset man who looked to be in his fifties drank from his canteen.

"If it's all the same to everyone, I'd like to get home. I wanted to ride with ya'll on account of my long friendship with Calvin. But every bone in my body is achin' an' we only been out here a few hours."

"No one'll blame you for leavin', Buck. You get back home safe, now."

"Thanks, Sheriff."

Buck turned his horse back toward town and trotted away.

"Okay, Bob, you come with me. You two," he pointed to the men standing near the campfire, take the north tracks. We don't have a lot of supplies, just enough for a few days. I want you all back in town, the beginning of next week with some prisoners or a report. Don't try bein' a hero—none of you. No amount of money is worth gettin' killed for."

All the men nodded.

After Doyle climbed back in his saddle, he smiled at Roxy. "This shouldn't take more than a day or two. They couldn't have gotten too far last night. An' there's always one thing you can count on slowin' a man down or stoppin' him dead in his tracks."

"What's that?" Roxy asked.

"Greed," Doyle told her. "If it ain't about a woman, it's always about money. Those are the two things a man will die for."

Roxy knew her father was right.

With the sun on her face, Roxy was enjoying the ride. It didn't matter to her if the money was retrieved. With her father beside her she felt safe, and because of his excellent tracking skills, all she had to do was follow his lead.

* * *

They had ridden for another two hours when they decided to rest and water their horses in a clearing. As Roxy climbed down from her horse, she saw something sparkling in the snow. Bending to have a closer look, she spotted Violet's heart-shaped necklace.

"What ya got there?" Doyle asked as he came up behind his daughter.

Roxy held the necklace out for him to see.

"Will you look at that," he said. "It appears one part of your problem took care of itself. When we get back to town, I can have Santa take it over to the Dunham girl."

"And how will you explain where it came from?" Roxy asked.

"Don't have a clue. But we got a lot of miles and time to figure it all out."

Chapter Twenty

"I tell ya Stony, it ain't here," Vernon said as he rifled through his saddlebag.

"How the hell can you keep gettin' more stupid? Every damn day you lose more of your brains."

"Shut up an' help me look!" Vernon shouted to his partner.

"That necklace was supposed to be part of our take. You said it was worth more than what Hank was gonna give us. You said that, remember you tellin' me that you know what real diamonds and rubies look like. Remember?"

"Course I remember, fool."

Vernon emptied the contents of both saddlebags across the bed and clawed through the items, sure he had overlooked the necklace the first time through.

Stony picked up one of the worn bags and stuck his finger through several of the holes along the bottom.

"Lookee here, fool. These bags ain't good for nothin'"

"I was gonna buy me some new ones with my share of the money," Vernon said meekly.

The couple that they had tied up and put in the closet kicked at the door.

"Shut up in there or we'll kill you both!" Stony shouted.

"No killin'," Vernon said. "Hank didn't want no one killed."

"Then why did he blast that man in the bank?" Stony asked.

Vernon shrugged. "He was just in the way, I guess."

"Pack all your shit up an' we'll go see what kinda food they got in the kitchen."

"But, Stony, what about the necklace?"

"Ain't nothin' we can do about it now. We need supplies an' I'm starvin'."

* * *

"So whoever robbed the bank, an' killed Cal Stern, snatched the necklace as well," Doyle said.

"Looks like it," Roxy said.

"How much do you suppose it's worth?"

"Sam never told me. He just said it belonged to his mother and he wanted his daughter to have it."

"How long have you known this man?" Doyle asked.

Roxy was embarrassed to tell her father that she hardly knew Sam Dunham at all. Their first meeting had led to sex, and when she promised to deliver the necklace, it was only because of the attraction and desire she felt at the time.

"Not very long."

"Well, word around town is that he beat his wife. He never laid a hand on you, did he?"

Roxy wasn't used to having a protector. "No, he was always kind and gentle."

"If I ever hear about him harming one hair on your head, I'll . . ."

She touched his arm. "I'm pretty good at taking care of myself."

"I know. But now that we're together again, you can always count on me to watch out for you. I have so many years to make up for."

She had never expected to see such guilt in his eyes when she was looking for him all those years. She wanted there to be callousness or indifference, something she could strike back at with the anger she carried. But guilt was something that made her pity him. It also made her feel cruel.

"Come on, she said. We have to keep going while it's light."

She carefully wrapped the necklace in the extra scarf in the saddlebag, tucked it deep down inside where it couldn't work its way loose. There would be no losing it again.

* * *

Ezra Brown and Colton Peterson had been sitting in Big Bertha's Saloon when all the commotion started. Christmas didn't mean much to them since both men lived alone and had no family to speak of. They met while working in the post office and became friends. But each lamented the dullness of their lives in Nebraska. So when they heard that the bank had been robbed, neither could resist running to see the excitement.

And when the sheriff called for volunteers to make up a posse, Ezra and Colton immediately joined in the hunt for the bank robbers. The three or four beers that they had consumed helped to bolster their courage.

The big house stood alone in the middle of the snowy prairie, beckoning to the two men who were cold and needed to rest. Hoping that a little Christmas cheer would be spread their way, they got off their horses and walked up to the front door.

At first they knocked on the door with their knuckles. When no one answered, they tried the brass knocker attached to the large front door.

"Someone's got to be home," Ezra said. "There's two horses tied out front and tracks going around to the back."

"Maybe we should try out there."

The men walked around the house. Approaching the back door they knocked, more loudly this time.

"Looks like no one's home," Colton said.

"You give up too easy, friend," Ezra said and pounded on the door with his fist.

"Hello!" Colton yelled. "We're with the posse lookin' for them bank robbers. Maybe you heard about what happened in town?"

The men were about to leave when a rifle blasted the door to splinters. The second shot cut Ezra down where he stood.

Colton couldn't move. When he saw the shooter kick the remainder of the door down and point his gun at him, he ran.

Chapter Twenty-One

Roxy wasn't sure if the bloody heap on the trail was an animal or human. Doyle saw the thing the same time and kicked his horse into a gallop to see what it was. His first instinct was to shield his daughter from the body, but she was next to him in a flash.

"It's Colton Peterson," he told Roxy. "Works down at the post office."

"Was he one of the posse?" Roxy asked.

"If I remember right, he was. Him and his friend, Ezra."

Colton reached out and touched Roxy's boot.

"Poor fella's still alive," Doyle whispered.

Roxy knelt down. "Who did this to you?"

"In the house . . . a big house."

"Ain't no house as near as I can see," Doyle said.

Colton pointed toward the north.

Roxy touched the man's forehead, realizing there was really nothing she could do for him.

"Ezra's dead. They killed him first," Colton Peterson said with his last breath.

Roxy stood up. "We'll have to take him back to town."

"I got a blanket with me," Doyle told her and went to get it from his horse.

They wrapped the man in the blanket and laid him across the saddle of his horse.

Roxy grabbed the reins then led the animal to where her horse stood, nervously jabbing the ground with his right hoof.

"Guess we better find that house."

* * *

"Jesus Christ, Stony! You went an' killed them men. What the hell did you do that for?"

"You heard 'em, they was with the posse. They was gonna bring us to jail or hang us right here on the spot. And this way there ain't no witnesses. We can ride outta here free as you please."

"Oh yeah? What about them people upstairs? They seen us. They'll tell the sheriff."

"Stop jabberin' at me. I haffta have somethin' to eat an' sit to think."

There was no reasoning with the man. Vernon knew from years of working side-by-side next to Stony, that when he had his mind set on something—right or wrong—there was no talking him out of it.

From the looks of things, the couple must have just returned from a Christmas dinner when Stony and Vernon forced their way inside. A Christmas dinner at someone else's home from the lack of food in the kitchen.

Lifting a checkered napkin, Vernon found a few slices of turkey next to a pile of mashed potatoes. Hardly enough to feed two grown men. Checking the small pantry, he found a loaf of bread and a jar of strawberry preserves.

"Well, we won't starve."

"An' we won't have enough to take with us," Stony complained. "How are we supposed to keep goin' on no food?"

Vernon ignored his companion and looked for two plates so he could divide the leftovers between them. Half a bottle of wine was in a cabinet and the men took turns passing it back and forth.

"So what are we gonna do about them?" Vernon asked.

"About who?"

"Them folks upstairs." Vernon looked up at the ceiling.

"Now you went an' spoiled my dinner," Stony said. "I almost forgot all about them."

"Well, I think we should just git outta here. They was so scared, they'll never remember nothin' about us," Vernon said.

"Are you crazy? They ain't gonna forget how two gunmen broke into their house, tied 'em up and locked 'em in a closet. Not to mention hearin' us shoot a coupla lawmen. An' if they got real bad memories, there's a gallon of blood out there to remind 'em. An' right in the middle is a body that's gettin' stiff as we speak."

"But I didn't kill no one," Vernon whined. "It was all you, Stony. You know it was."

"No one else knows that 'cept the two of us. So, friend, if I go to jail because of your big mouth, you're comin' along with me."

Vernon jumped up and pulled his gun out, holding it on Stony.

"No! I'm not killin' no one. I'm done here. Now stand up."

Stony started to laugh at the sudden backbone Vernon was showing. But when he saw the rage in the man's eyes, he stood up.

"Now go outside an' git up on yer horse."

"But my gear's upstairs."

"Okay then, we'll both go an' git our things. But after that, I never wanna see yer sorry face again."

Vernon motioned for Stony to start walking with the gun in his hand.

Following the killer down the hall, Vernon prayed he could get out of there unharmed. If only Stony would take his saddlebags and leave, peacefully. But when they came to the bottom of a staircase, Stony quickly spun around, grabbed Vernon's right hand and wrenched the gun out of it.

"Now you march up there. It'll be just as easy to git rid of three of you as it would be for two." He laughed.

Vernon walked slowly, even though Stony kept jabbing the barrel of the gun into his back.

"What the hell happened to you, Stony? I thought you was in this just for the money, like me. How come you all of a sudden like killin' so much?"

"I like the power, Vern. It's always been about power. The man with a gun is the big man. He's respected."

They were almost to the bedroom door when they heard horses approaching.

Chapter Twenty-Two

"Well," Doyle said, "this has to be the house. There's not another one for miles."

"No sign of anything wrong in the front. I'll check the back."

Roxy tied off her horse as well as the one carrying Colton Peterson and walked around the house.

The snow was red with blood. Bits of wood from where the back door had been blasted stuck in the ground. Three horses were in a small stable a few yards from the main house.

Doyle came around the corner and was startled at the sight.

"God, Almighty," he said looking at the remains of Ezra Brown. "Poor bastard."

Thinking of the three horses, Roxy realized the bank robbers were probably still inside and grabbed Doyle's arm, yanking him into the stable.

"From the looks of it, I'd say there are two of them."

"Probably holding the family at gunpoint . . . if they're still alive," Doyle said. "We gotta flush 'em out."

"They probably saw us ride up," Roxy said. "The longer we stay out here the more time we're giving them to think about it."

"Are you ready?" Doyle asked.

"Yes, I am," she told her father.

The duo reached for their guns at the same time and crept along the walls of the stable.

"Come outta there!" Gavin Doyle shouted. "Now!"

They were answered with a flurry of bullets.

Neither Roxy nor Doyle fired back, afraid they might hit an innocent . . .

* * *

Stony shouted to Vernon to open the closet and bring out the couple tied up inside.

Vernon unlocked the door, then pulled the woman by her long hair with one hand and the man by the collar of his shirt with his other hand. He'd hoped both people could escape this whole mess without being harmed, but if someone had to die inside the house, better them than himself.

"What you want me to do with 'em, Stony?"

"Bring 'em near the window."

Breaking the glass with his gun, Stony shouted down toward the stable.

"I got the owners of this here house if you'd care to do some target shootin'!"

* * *

"Steady," Doyle told Roxy. "Just wait til you can get a clean shot."

Roxy nodded.

When there was no response, Stony grabbed the woman away from Vernon's grip and pushed her face through the broken window. She screamed as the glass cut her face.

"Leave her be an' just walk out the front door," Doyle called to them.

"You expect me to believe that yer just gonna let us walk outta here? You must think my brain don't work all that good."

In the beginning, Roxy was just happy she had gotten the necklace back and didn't really care about the bank's money. And every minute she rode with her father was a happy one. But once she'd looked into Colton's eyes and then saw the body of Ezra Brown, she got angry. Now there was a terrified woman being tortured by a pair of killers and she could only think of the injustice.

"Let him go!" the woman cried from the window. "My husband and I just want to be left alone."

"There's a husband up there, too," Roxy said to Doyle. "So how are we gonna tell the good man from the bad?"

"He'll show himself. They always do."

Vernon pulled the husband toward the window the way he'd seen Stony do, but the man was bigger and stronger than the robber. He'd been able to untie his hands while with his wife and brought back his fist, landing a punch so heavy that it knocked Vernon off his feet.

Hearing the commotion, Stony turned around to have a look. When he saw what had happened, he brought his gun up to the woman's temple.

"How'd you like yer pretty little wife to git her head blown off?"

"No! Don't hurt her!"

Taking her chance, Roxy shot the man in the back when he turned away from the window.

The woman fell to the floor and crawled to her husband, sobbing hysterically.

For one moment, Vernon held his gun and aimed it at the couple. But then he saw Stony lying dead on the floor and thought better of it.

"I never killed no one," he said, falling on his knees. "Don't shoot me; I never hurt no one. All I ever wanted was the money."

After picking up Vernon's gun the husband ran to the window.

"It's okay. We're okay now!"

Roxy and Doyle ran for the backdoor and hurried up the stairs.

Chapter Twenty-Three

They made a peculiar sight, the four of them riding back toward Lincoln that way. Roxy on Nona, guiding Colton Peterson's horse which held the man's dead body. Gavin Doyle led the way, riding high in his saddle, pulling along Vernon's horse, the robber's hands tied to the saddle horn.

The couple back at the big house said they would bury Stony and Ezra in the snow until the sheriff or family decided what they wanted done with the bodies.

* * *

Sheriff Lloyd North turned the key on Vernon's cell.

"You two had quite a day," he said as he walked to his office where Doyle and Roxy were sitting. "You got back some of the bank money, brought in one of the robbers and saved a coupla people."

"And thank God it's over. I'm gettin' too old for this bull," Doyle sighed.

The sheriff turned to Roxy. "I see why they write about you, Miss Doyle. You're a very brave woman."

Then to her father he said, "You got some daughter there. Should be mighty proud."

"I am," Doyle said, smiling.

"The bounty hunter came long before Lady Gunsmith," Roxy told them.

"Sure, but I ain't never seen no dime novel about his exploits."

"Maybe not," Roxy said, "but . . ."

"We're both proud of each other," Doyle interrupted. "Now that we're done pattin' ourselves on the back, let's figure out what's next."

The sheriff walked over to the wall behind his desk and ripped off a wanted poster. He tossed it to Doyle.

"We're not done—I'm not done with this—until the rest of the money's returned. I don't expect either of you to stay in town; you've already done more than I asked. But there's a fat reward for the leader of the gang. Dead or alive."

"And just who is he?" Roxy asked.

"Goes by lotsa names, but he was born, David Middleton. Nowadays he calls himself Henry Shepherd. A no-good, who started off stealin' horses. Looks like he's moved on to robbin' banks. And killin'."

Roxy studied the poster for a moment then turned toward Doyle.

"This is the man we saw in Big Bertha's. The tall man with the dark beard. Remember you told me how you put him in jail?"

"You've come across Shepherd before?" the sheriff asked.

"A time or two."

"Then you might have some knowledge of his habits? Or maybe his weaknesses?" The sheriff looked hopefully in Doyle's direction.

"All I know is the man's a killer. He'll do anything to get what he wants whether it's a horse or money. An' from what we've seen, his men are just as ruthless."

Roxy laughed. "Well, except for that one in there." She pointed to the cellblock.

"I'm sure I can scare some information outta him," Sheriff North said. "But that'll have to wait until tomorrow."

Doyle stood up. "My bones are achin' for a nice bed an' some sleep. Come on, Roxy, I'll walk you home." He reached down and took her hand. "And I'll let you know what I'm gonna do tomorrow, Sheriff."

"Good enough," North said. "Oh . . . Merry Christmas, a day late."

* * *

As they walked out of the sheriff's office, the wind picked up. Roxy pulled the collar of her jacket up to cover her ears.

She stopped and stood in front of him. "I don't even know where you live."

"It always changes. Sometimes I climb into Bertha's bed, other times I hold up in a cabin outside of town. But most times, I'm at Arlene's place. My job makes me a lot of enemies. Angry children of men I hauled to jail, crazy wives, especially partners who got double-crossed or cheated. Too many people who want me dead."

"I've had a few of those come after me, too."

"So it's better if I take you back to the Baron House where you'll be safe."

"So safe, that someone got into my room and stole that necklace," she reminded him.

"Well, you got it back. I'm sure Mr. Clark has a strongbox you can use. And I know for sure that you can take care of yourself."

"But, Dad . . ."

"Look, the less you know about my whereabouts, the safer you are, Roxy girl."

"Well," she relented, "you have managed to stay alive all these years. But we can have breakfast tomorrow morning, right?"

"I wouldn't miss it."

"Is eight o'clock good?" Roxy asked.

"Great. Meet me at the Cornhusker Café."

"With bells on."

Roxy kissed Doyle on the cheek and went into the Baron House.

* * *

With one hand holding the key and the other on her gun, Roxy Doyle slowly entered her room. The curtains were slightly parted, letting in enough light that she could get to the lamp on a table and light it. She was slightly nervous until she saw the basket of cookies Matilda must have brought up.

After inspecting the sitting room, then the bedroom, she took off her jacket and went to the closet to hang it up.

When the man jumped out, Roxy went for her gun, "Whoa! It's me . . . Sam. Don't shoot," He laughed as he held up his hands.

Chapter Twenty-Four

"Sam! You scared me half to death." Roxy put the gun next to the lamp and let Sam sweep her into his arms.

"Oh God, Roxy, I missed you so much."

He held her tight and then started kissing her neck.

"But it's only been a few days."

Nuzzling her shoulder he asked, "You didn't miss me?"

So many questions spun around in her head. Was this person really as violent as the gossip she'd heard? Or was he the charming man she'd volunteered to help? Could she trust him? And what was it about his telegram that made her uneasy? She hardly knew him.

But as his fingers unbuttoned her shirt and then he tugged at her belt . . .

"Sam, I just got off the trail. I'm dirty. Hold up a minute."

He licked between her breasts.

"I like my women salty," he said, and they both laughed.

Her resistance was wearing down as he squeezed her nipples. And when he carried her over to the bed, she had to have him on top of her, inside her.

Their clothes came off in a flurry until both were naked. He rolled onto the bed, holding her tightly against him while she clawed at his back from the desire she felt boiling up inside her.

Roxy Doyle had her fair share of men since becoming a woman. But Sam Dunham fired her up like no other had. Just the thought of him made her burn between her legs. When she was with him, he could talk her into doing anything. Just the way he said her name stirred something deep inside her body. But she knew for a fact that it wasn't love. Love felt more warm and comfortable. No, this was lust, pure and simple. And for as long as it would last, she was going to enjoy every moment with him.

His hair fell in soft waves to his shoulders. She tangled her fingers in the blonde locks and forced his mouth to hers. Their kisses went from soft quickly to hard and frantic. She wanted to devour him and glide her tongue deep into his mouth. Spreading her legs, she sat in his lap on the mattress.

When he couldn't stand it anymore, Sam got on top of her while Roxy grabbed his butt and pulled him into her. They pounded away at each other in a steady rhythm for a good five minutes, neither wanting to stop the delicious heat between them. Sweat glistened on their chests and trickled down to their bellies.

"I love you, Roxy," Sam whispered into her ear. "I loved you the moment I saw you."

It was all happening too fast to suit her, but she didn't want the passion surging through her to ever stop.

So she lied and said, "I love you, too."

Those words seemed to excite him even more, and he withdrew his penis then positioned himself between her thighs so he could lick her pussy. Roxy thought she would go insane with the intense pleasure.

Passionate moans increased until the sounds she made were foreign to her. It was as if there was an animal inside screaming to be released. The room started to shift. Instead of being frightened of losing the control she always held, she closed her eyes and floated along a wave of feelings she never had before.

Just when she thought there wasn't anything left in her, Sam poked a finger inside her vagina, and everything started to spin. She covered her mouth with one hand, not wanting any of the hotel guests to hear her. Then a burning sensation roared through her stomach and rushed out of her body.

Sam realized that Roxy was spent, but he had no intention of letting her go just yet. "Oh no," he said, "we're not done,"

Could someone die from lust? she wondered.

She was exhausted and lay listless for a minute, but then Sam climbed on top of her and pushed his manhood deeper inside her until all she wanted was for him to never let her go. Never.

He was so consumed with her, so focused on his pleasure now that she'd found hers that he moved quicker. Grinding away, in and out, in and out.

Roxy got her second wind and moved her hips with renewed energy. The sheets beneath them were damp with their juices. She could hear the mantle clock in the other room ticking along with their passion.

Finally, Sam was nearing his release while Roxy was feeling another wave of pleasure move from her stomach down into her legs. The couple grabbed each other tightly as they cried out their pleasure in unison.

* * *

"You told me you were afraid to come to town because of Sheriff North." Roxy reminded him. "So what changed your mind?" And how did he know which hotel she was staying at? She wondered but didn't ask.

"I heard about the robbery and figured I could get to Lincoln while the sheriff was busy." He sat on the edge of the bed. "Why the questions? Aren't you glad to see me?"

"Of course I am," Roxy said. "But like I told you in the telegram, I found my father and have been spending time with him. We have a lot to catch up on."

"I know," Sam said. "But I had to find out how Violet liked the necklace. She did get it, didn't she?"

"Well," Roxy started, "that's a whole 'nother story."

Chapter Twenty-Five

"An' just where did you meet this fella?" Doyle asked Roxy as they ate breakfast the next morning.

"I was in Omaha . . . looking for you . . ."

"I had just left. Guess that's the closest we've come to reuniting."

"No, there were a few times I just missed you. Even a time or two when I was told you were dead."

"You poor kid," Doyle said and looked at his daughter with sad eyes. "You've got to believe I was never intentionally runnin' away from you. As far as I knew, when I left, you were being well cared for. Every month I sent money for you."

"Well, I never got any of it," Roxy said. She put down her fork and picked up the coffee cup next to her plate. "Dad, it wasn't your fault. You did your best." Then as she drank, she studied his weathered face.

Doyle shook his head slowly, "I'm not so sure about that, honey."

They sat quietly for a moment.

"So, did you tell Sam all about the necklace being stolen?" Doyle continued.

"No," Roxy said.

"Why not?"

Roxy picked up a biscuit and spread honey on the warm bread.

"Dad, when you hunt down a man, do you follow his trail or your gut feelings more?"

"At first it was just horse or wagon markings in the dirt or snow or water. But I got to be this age by tryin' to think like another man. Tryin' to outsmart him, not out ride him."

"That's what Clint Adams told me. He said I should trust my instincts."

"So, what does all this have to do with Sam Dunham?"

Roxy swallowed her biscuit. "Something just ain't right."

"So you're sayin' that you never told him about the necklace? He thinks his daughter has it? Did you tell him that I—ahh Santa—gave it to the girl?"

"That's the strange part," Roxy said. "I told him the gift was stolen and he just shrugged. I apologized for not getting it to Violet and he said it wasn't my fault and not to worry."

"So now what are you gonna do with it?"

"It's in the hotel, wrapped real good. Mr. Clark, the manager, put it in his strongbox. He never asked what it was, just locked it up."

"Huh," Doyle said. "You can tell Mr. Dunham his bauble is safe later, after you know him better, I guess."

"That's what I was thinking."

"So where is this fella of yours?

"In the hotel, in my room," Roxy said. "But I don't know how he found me; I never told him the hotel I was at."

"Come on, Roxy, girl, you're famous, remember? All Mr. Dunham had to do was follow the gossip."

"You're probably right."

They were on their second cup of coffee when they saw Sheriff North walk across the room toward them.

"I've been lookin' all over town for you two. Mind if I sit?"

"Course not, Sheriff," Roxy said. "Have you had breakfast?'

"Oh, hours ago, don't worry about me. I came to ask you two some questions about the shootin' out at the Elrod place."

"We never knew their name," Doyle said.

"Nice couple," North said. "Moved out here in the Spring. But after what happened, they're talking about goin' back East."

"I don't blame them," Roxy said.

The sheriff scooted his chair closer to the table. "I was wonderin' if you two would kindly come by my office later. There are some loose ends to tie up."

"Sure thing," Doyle said. "With all of us goin' after them men, I was curious about comparin' stories."

"Good. How about stoppin' by in an hour? That should give you enough time to finish up here."

Before Doyle or Roxy could answer, the sheriff stood up and walked out of the café.

"I was goin' to drop in on the sheriff even without him askin'."

Roxy nodded. "When he went west, looking for the robbers, we never heard what he and the others found."

"Or didn't find."

Chapter Twenty-Six

Roxy and Gavin Doyle entered Sheriff North's office a couple of hours later. During that time Roxy talked about something that had occurred to her when she got away from Sam Dunham and his hands weren't on her. That was the only time she was able to think straight.

"What's on your mind, Roxy girl?" Doyle asked before they left the café after breakfast.

"We rode out with a posse of seven. Right?"

"Right."

"One man headed back to town when we found the three sets of tracks."

"So?" Doyle asked.

"So the sheriff took Bob and followed one set of tracks; you and I followed another set. Ezra and Colton followed a third."

"And there were three sets of tracks. One belonged to the two we caught. Another belonged to Hank."

"So who did the other tracks belong to if there were only three bank robbers?" Roxy said.

Doyle finally got it.

"I'm gettin' slow in my old age," he said. "There were four men."

"Okay, so we saw three men in the saloon. They must've had a lookout outside," she said.

"Or Hank and the other two pulled the job, but somebody else planned it."

They stared across the table at each other, then stood up.

"Let's go see what the sheriff thinks of this," he said, and they left . . .

* * *

They took the time to give the lawman their statements approaching him with their theories.

"I was actually having the same thoughts," he said, when they finished. "There's got to be another bank robber who got away with Hank."

"And," Roxy said, "we only recovered some of the money."

"So these two have to be out there, with most of the money," Doyle said.

"Unless," Roxy said, "they doubled back on us."

"You think they might still be in town?" Sheriff North asked.

"Could be," she said.

"Let's see what we can find out from Vernon," the sheriff said.

* * *

In the cell block all three faced Vernon through the bars. Roxy and Doyle allowed the sheriff to start the questioning.

"As far as I knew, there was three of us," Vernon said, "me, Stony and Hank."

"And Hank was the boss?" North asked.

"Yes," Vernon said. "I mean, I took orders from Stony, and he took orders from Hank."

"And Hank planned the bank job?"

"Yes."

"Why did you kill the banker?"

"I didn't kill anybody," Vernon said. "The banker wasn't supposed to be there, and when he saw him, Hank shot 'im. Then when we got to that house Stony decided to kill those people. I think Stony just liked killing."

"Where's the money?" North asked.

"Well, we stopped to split the take. At least, I thought we did. We unwrapped the money and burned the bank bands, but then Hank put all the money into his saddlebag and said we wasn't dividin' the take, not on the trail. He said we was splittin' up, and we'd settle up the money later. He told me and Stony to keep ridin'."

"And what was he going to do?" Doyle asked.

"That's when I found out there was a fourth man. Hank was gonna wait and see him."

"What was his part in all this?" North asked.

"I ain't sure," Vernon said, "but I think he was Hank's boss."

"I thought Hank was the boss," North said.

"So did I," Vernon said. "Believe me, I'm as confused as you are."

"Vernon, are Hank and the other man back in town?"

"I dunno. But as far as I know, they got the money."

"But you never saw the fourth man?" Roxy asked.

"I never did," Vernon said. "I didn't even know about him until after the job."

"All right," North said. "Just siddown and shut up."

North looked at Roxy and Doyle, and then they left the cell block.

"I didn't kill nobody!" Vernon shouted. "I really didn't. Hey, can I get some food?"

"I'll feed you in due time," the sheriff shouted back.

North closed the door of the cell block and locked it.

"You should let him go hungry," Roxy said.

"I can't do that," the sheriff said. "I'm supposed to keep my prisoners fed. But don't worry, the place where I get the food isn't very good."

Chapter Twenty-Seven

"We've got to find out if those other two are in town," Sheriff North said, as they left the office. "If they are, we have to find them. If they're not, I'll take another, better outfitted posse." He looked directly at Doyle. "I could use your help, Mr. Doyle. You're an expert tracker."

"I am, indeed, and you've got it, Sheriff."

"Me, too," Roxy said, even though the man hadn't asked her. Roxy thought the man still didn't think a woman's place was in a posse.

"Thank you, uh, both," North said.

"I'm gonna go out and look around, and then check in on my wife and daughter."

"We'll walk around, as well, and see what we can find," Doyle said.

"I'll meet you back here in a while and compare notes," North said. "If we don't find out anythin' we'll ride out tomorrow."

"And you *will* be able to put together a better equipped posse?" Doyle asked.

"I believe so," North said. "I'll have someone who can sit here with the prisoner until we get back."

Doyle looked at Roxy and said, "Let's see what we can find out."

They left the office and started toward Roxy's hotel.

"Where do you want to start?" she asked.

"The fact that we found that necklace out in the snow leads to a question."

"I know," Roxy said. "Is Sam Dunham involved in the robbery."

"I'm glad you're able to think that way," Doyle said.

"Why wouldn't I?" she asked.

"Well, you're emotionally involved."

"So you're thinkin' that Sam is the fourth man," Roxy said to her father.

"Aren't you?" he asked. "He sent you to Lincoln with that necklace, supposedly to give it to his daughter. Why would those two steal it from your room and take it with them?"

"I don't know," she said. "But we could look at the necklace as a condition between them."

"So, he used you to get the necklace into town, but knew you'd never get the chance to give it to his daughter."

Roxy wondered if the man she had spent so many pleasant hours with was not the true Sam Dunham. Rather he was the man the sheriff and his wife had described to her. She hadn't even seen an ounce of cruelty in the man, but perhaps he was playing her to get her to deliver the necklace to Lincoln.

"Let's get a cup of coffee," she said to her father. "I want to talk about something."

* * *

They stopped in the café and took a table in the back. When they each had a cup, she told Doyle as much as she dared. If she told him all of it, he might kill Dunham.

"So, if you don't think he's the man you think he is, but rather who the sheriff and his wife said he was— maybe you should tell the sheriff he's in town and that you suspect him of being involved with the bank robbery."

"It's not so much that I suspect him, but I'm afraid he pulled the wool over my eyes."

"No one likes bein' made a fool of."

"I'm going to have to find out for sure," Roxy said.

"And how will you do that?" Doyle asked.

"Easy," she said. "I'm going to ask him."

"Ask him if he's a bank robber?"

"Yes."

"And you think he'll tell you the truth."

"I don't know what kind of man he really is," Roxy said, "but if he's like most men, he'll be arrogant enough to talk."

"I know what kind of man his daughter wants him to be," Doyle said. "She asked Santa to bring her father back to live with them."

"Poor Violet," Roxy said. "Her mother and stepfather will never let that happen."

"I'll come with you, Roxy," Doyle said.

"No, Dad," Roxy said. "That wouldn't end well."

"It'll end fine," her father said." I'll thrash him to within an inch of his life, and he'll confess to you."

"That's what I'm afraid you'll do," she said.

Chapter Twenty-Eight

Doyle reluctantly let Roxy go to talk with Sam Dunham on her own. As she headed for her hotel, Doyle returned to the sheriff's office, hoping to still find him there.

"Back already?" North said, surprised. "Did you find out somethin'?"

"Maybe."

"Where?"

"From Roxy," Doyle said.

"What did she say?"

"You know Sam Dunham, of course."

"I do," North said. "He's my stepdaughter's father, and a nasty man. What's he got to do with this?"

"What do you think?"

"I didn't think he was involved at all. Does your daughter think he is?"

"She thinks he might be."

"Why?"

Doyle told North about the necklace.

"That's what was stolen from her room?"

"Yes."

"And you found it on the trail?"

"We did."

"I don't understand what this necklace has to do with anything."

"He says it was for his daughter. Roxy wanted me to give it to Violet."

"I see," North said. "Why would your daughter do this for him? How does she know him?"

"She met him in Omaha. They . . . spent some time together, and he asked her for a favor."

"Oh, I get it now," North said. "He's a handsome man. A woman can fall in love with him if she doesn't know his true nature. I know he's a nasty man, but I never thought he was a lawbreaker."

"Roxy's not in love with him, but I think she was infatuated enough to agree to deliver the necklace."

"But if he wanted her to give it to Violet, why did those men steal it?"

"I can't figure that out," Doyle said, "but Roxy's askin' him right now."

"Does she think he'll tell her?"

"She thinks she can figure him out."

"I doubt that," North said, "especially if she's sweet on him. So, you're tellin' me he's in town. Where is she meetin' him?"

"I don't know."

"Her room?"

"She didn't say."

"If we go there now, we might catch them together."

"And there might be some shooting," Doyle said, "Do you want to be responsible for killin' your stepdaughter's father?"

"No," he said, "but I can't let him get away with this."

"I suggest you let Roxy have her way and see what she can find out."

"And if he's guilty of robbin' the bank, she'll turn 'im over to me?"

"You bet," Doyle said. "My girl is a law abidin' citizen. Besides, if he tried to use her, she's gonna be real mad."

"All right, Mr. Doyle," North said, "we'll do it your way, for now. When will we know?"

"When I hear somethin' from her, you'll be the first to know."

"I better be," North said. "If Sam Dunham's behind this, I want him."

Chapter Twenty-Nine

Roxy found Sam Dunham reclining on the bed in her room.

"There you are," he said, smiling with his hands behind his head. "I missed you."

He stood up and started to remove his shirt. He had a beautiful body, but she had to resist him.

"Don't," she told him, "I want to talk."

"You haven't preferred to talk much before this," Sam said. He put his shirt back on. "What's on your mind?"

"Why are you in Lincoln, Sam?" she asked. "You asked me to bring the necklace here, and now you're here. Why would you take that chance?"

"I wasn't gonna come, but then I realized how much I wanted to see Violet."

"And have you seen her?"

"From a distance," he said. "I haven't let her see me."

"Did you hear about the bank robbery in town?"

"I did," he said. "The bank manager was killed. That's a horrible thing."

"There were supposed to be three men involved, but when I joined the posse, we found tracks left by four."

"Is that right?" Dunham said. "Who was the fourth?"

"Nobody knows," Roxy said. "Well, one man knows, but we don't have him."

"Do you think the remaining two men are in town?"

"Could be."

"Why would they come back if they've already robbed the bank?"

"I don't know," Roxy said. "We saw some tracks coming back. They must have a reason for returning."

"Are you still gonna look for them?" Dunham asked. "And leave me all alone?"

"My father and I have promised to stay with the sheriff's posse."

"That's Sheriff North, right? Violet's stepfather?"

"That's right."

Dunham shook his head.

"I hate losin' another girl to that man."

"You haven't lost this girl," Roxy said. "But I have some questions for you, Sam."

Dunham sat on the bed, again.

"Go ahead and ask."

"Why are you here?" Roxy asked.

"Don't you believe I'm here because I missed you?" he asked.

"Not at all," she said.

Dunham laughed.

"So do you believe I'm here because of the bank?"

"I'm afraid of that, Sam."

"Why would I come back if I already robbed it?" he asked her.

"Because you have some unfinished business."

"Like what?"

"Your daughter, your ex-wife, the sheriff. Who knows? Something else?"

Dunham laughed and shook his head.

"Why would I risk fifty-thousand dollars by coming back here once I had it?"

"Who said there was fifty-thousand dollars in that bank?" Roxy asked.

Dunham's face fell for a moment before he regained control.

"A bank that size . . ." He got off the bed. "Never mind. I'm out of the mood, Roxy. Maybe next time we see each other you won't be so suspicious, and we can resume our . . . fun."

As he started for the door Roxy said, "Sam!"

He stopped with his hand on the doorknob.

"Yes?"

"Did you have something to do with robbing that bank?"

"Would you believe me if I said no?"

"Probably not."

Dunham smiled.

"We'll see each other again, Roxy. And don't think about trying to stop me from leaving. You're fast, but not that fast."

He went out the door and she let him leave.

* * *

"Why'd you let him go?" Sheriff North asked.

"I couldn't be sure he was involved."

"Are you sure it wasn't because he's so handsome?"

"Easy, Sheriff," Doyle said. "My daughter wouldn't let a man go if she knew he was guilty of bank robbery and murder. Besides, Vernon told us Hank killed the bank manager."

"If the four men robbed the bank, they're all also guilty of murder."

"If I get proof he did it," Roxy said, "I'll bring him in."

"We're all gonna bring him in," North said. "I always knew he was bad to the bone. I just feel sorry for Violet. She loves her daddy."

The office door opened, and a tall string bean of a man came in.

"This is Thad," Sheriff North said. "He keeps an eye on the office. Thad this is Gavin Doyle and his daughter, Roxy."

Thad's eyes were opened wide as he looked at Roxy, even before she was introduced to him.

"The Lady Gunsmith?" he said, in wonder.

"They're part of my posse," North said. "We're gonna be lookin' around town for those bank robbers, and some more possemen."

"But they already robbed the bank," Thad said. "Why would they still be here?"

"We're gonna find out. The prisoner's been fed."

"Yessir."

Sheriff North left the office with Roxy and Gavin Doyle.

Outside the door Roxy said, "Sheriff, do you know how much money was taken from the bank?"

"The assistant manager told me there was fifty-thousand in the safe. Why?"

She shrugged and said, "Just curious."

Chapter Thirty

North, Roxy and Doyle spent the afternoon making a complete circuit of the town. North recruited several men for his posse. Roxy kept an eye out for Sam Dunham, to see if he was with any other men. If he was, one of them might be Hank.

They stopped in Big Bertha's as it neared dusk.

When they were set up with a beer each at the bar, Doyle asked North, "How many did you recruit?"

"With us I've got seven. That should be enough to hunt two." He looked at Roxy. "Did you see Dunham?"

"No."

"I didn't, either. But at least you saw him in town today. Hank could be long gone with the bank money. We'll head out in the morning."

"And go which way?" Roxy asked. "How will you know what tracks to follow?"

"You forget," North said. "I'll have an expert tracker with me. I'll trust your father to figure out which tracks to follow. We can go back to that house we found Vernon in and go from there."

Roxy looked at her father, who shrugged and said, "I'll give it a try."

"We better get somethin' to eat, and then some rest," North said. "I'm gonna check the office, and then head home. You're both welcome to come eat with us."

Doyle saw Big Bertha coming down from upstairs.

"I think I can take care of myself right here," Doyle said.

"Miss Doyle? My wife's a helluva cook."

"Thank you. I accept," Roxy said.

"We'll see you in the mornin' at my office, Doyle."

"Right."

" 'night, Dad,"

" 'night, Roxy girl."

As Sheriff North and Roxy took their leave, Big Bertha reached Doyle. He had watched her, a vision in lavender, all the way from across the floor.

"Good God, that's a beautiful girl," Bertha said. "You think she'd wanna work for me?"

"That's my daughter, Bertha," Doyle said, "and I doubt it."

"Any objection to me askin' 'er?"

"None. But it's a waste of time."

Bertha sighed.

"You're right," Bertha said, "a girl like her wouldn't work here on a bet."

"We'll be goin' out with a posse tomorrow," Doyle said.

"Still lookin' for the bank robbers?"

"Yep."

"I thought they were gone?"

"Might be, might not. We're keepin' an open mind."

"You lookin' for a place to spend the night?" Big Bertha asked.

"If it includes a meal," Doyle said.

She smiled.

"It includes a lot more than that."

"Then I'm all yours."

* * *

North and Roxy walked into the office and Thad stood up.

"How's the prisoner?" North asked.

"All quiet, sheriff," Thad said, still unable to take his eyes off Roxy.

"I'll be at my house the rest of the night," North said. "I'll need you here."

"Yessir," Thad said. "What about Miss Doyle? I could keep 'er company—"

"Relax, Thad," North said, patting the young man on the back "Miss Doyle is gonna eat with me and my family. We'll see you in the mornin'."

"Yessir."

151

The lawman and Roxy left the office.

* * *

"I hope I'm not imposing," Roxy said, when the sheriff told his wife she'd be having supper with them.

"Not at all," Julie insisted. "Violet would love to talk to you."

"She's a darling little girl," Roxy said. "I'd love to talk to her, too."

"Let's leave that until after supper," North said. "Right now, we can get cleaned up. You can hang your gun here with mine."

Roxy hesitantly took her gunbelt off, but finally figured she was okay in a lawman's house.

North allowed Roxy to wash up, first, then offered to help Julie while he got cleaned up.

Chapter Thirty-One

Violet was very excited to find Roxy Doyle sitting at the supper table with her and her family. She talked incessantly, asking Roxy all kinds of questions. After the first few moments, her parents stopped trying to quiet her, after Roxy told them she didn't mind.

"What's it like," Violet finally asked, "to have Santa Claus as a daddy?"

"Violet—" North said.

"No, it's all right," Roxy told the sheriff. "It's wonderful, Violet. Especially since I hadn't seen my daddy in such a long time. Probably since I was your age."

"I haven't seen my daddy in a long time, either," the little girl said.

"I'm sure he's out there, Violet, and he loves you."

"Oh, I know he is," the little girl said, "and I'm gonna see him soon."

"It's time to get ready for bed, Violet," Julie said.

"But we just ate," the child said.

"That's all right, honey, Julie said. "You can read for a while before you go to bed. But say goodnight to Miss Doyle now. She'll be leaving soon."

"Goodnight, Miss Doyle," Violet said. "I hope to see you again."

You will, honey," Roxy said. "You will."

Julie got up from the table with Violet.

"I'll see that Violet goes to her room and come back to make some coffee. Please don't leave."

"I won't," Roxy promised.

Julie took Violet to her room. The house was all on one floor and seemed to have two bedrooms.

"This is a nice house," Roxy said. "Is it yours or the town's?"

"The town gave it to us when they made me sheriff a couple of years ago," North said. "At the time I was already married to Julie. Dunham had left her and Violet the year before."

"When did Violet last see her father?" Roxy asked.

"Around that time," North said, "probably two years."

"What a shame," Roxy said. "Up until a few days ago I hadn't seen my father for many years. I hope Violet doesn't have to wait that long."

"I hope she does," North said. "Even longer. "I'm tryin' to fill that void."

"Then I hope you can do it."

"You obviously know Dunham, but you haven't yet seen the real Sam Dunham. You still see the charmer."

"I may already be disillusioned. I'm afraid he tried to use me."

"That's probably true," North said. "And he's probably already picked out a new playmate."

"Maybe," Roxy said, "that's how we can find him. By finding his new girl."

"That's an idea," North said.

They stopped talking about Dunham when Julie returned to the room and fetched the coffee and pie.

When they were all at the table with their dessert Julie said, "You didn't have to stop talking about Dunham when I came in. What's he up to now?"

"He's in town," Roxy said.

"Oh," Julie said, looking alarmed. "Does he want to see Violet?"

"Roxy and I are tryin' to figure out whether or not he was involved with the bank robbery."

"Oh my," Julie said. "I never expected Sam to go that bad,"

"He was that bad when you met him, Julie," North said, "only you never saw it."

"It's hard for a woman to see that part of a man she loves . . . until he forces her to stop loving him."

"I can understand you not wanting to see her father. But how will you explain it to her?" Roxy asked.

"I'll have to do that," North said, "after I've arrested him and put him away. I'll try to make her understand."

"But if he robbed the bank, then he was involved in killing the manager," Julie said. "He won't want to be taken in for murder. He'll make you kill him. How will you explain that to her?"

"I don't know," North said. "I want to take him and the others alive, but if he makes me kill him . . . I'll explain it, somehow."

After they finished their coffee and pie, Roxy said goodnight to Julie and thanked her for the meal.

"You can thank me by keeping my husband alive when you go out with the posse."

"I'll do my best."

North went out the door with Roxy.

"We should go looking for Dunham's next girl," North said.

"You can stay home, Sheriff," she said. "With that badge on, my father and I will have a better chance of finding her."

"And how will you do that?"

"I think," Roxy said, "my father has just the person to help us."

Chapter Thirty-Two

When Doyle and Big Bertha got to her suite of rooms she stood in the center, raised her arms above her head and allowed him to disrobe her. She knew Doyle loved looking at the luminous skin of her bodacious body.

When she was naked, he began kissing her shoulders and breasts, playfully nibbling her large nipples, until she sank to her knees in front of him, and lowered his trousers so that his hard cock sprang out at her. She took it into her hands, fondled and stroked it until it was rock hard, and then took it into her mouth, sucked and licked it like a hungry mule at a salt lick.

"Jesus, woman," he said. "You're gonna finish me right here."

She laughed, got to her feet and took hold of his cock with one hand.

"Not right here," she told him, "not with that big bed in the next room."

She tugged him to the bedroom, and he went quite willingly until they were on the bed, rolling about to-gether and then managed to pin her down and poke his cock into her wet, steamy depths . . .

* * *

"Oh God," she said, as they cuddled together, "what am I gonna do for this kind of attention when you're gone?"

"You'll have any number of volunteers, Bertha."

"Oh, not a lot of men appreciate a woman my size, Doyle. Not like you do."

"If that's true, it's because you're more woman than most men can handle."

"Even so, I'm not enough for you. You need to have both Arlene and me at your beck and call."

"Hardly my beck and call," he said. "I'm lucky either of you even give me the time of day."

"We both know what we have, Doyle," Bertha said. "You're a special man."

"Yeah, real special," he said. "A man who would leave his little girl behind."

"She looks like she grew up real good, Doyle," Bertha said. "And from what I can see, the little girl still loves her daddy."

"Yeah," Doyle said, "God only knows why."

"Because you're her daddy," she said. "I still love the memory of my father, and he was a real no-good sonofabitch."

"Well, Doyle said, "you seem to have grown up real good, too, Bertha."

"You came back with some of the bank robbers, didn't you?" Bertha asked, wanting to change the subject.

"One alive, one dead," Doyle said. "There might be two more."

"Why would they still be in town?" she asked. "They got the money."

"Hidin' in plain sight, maybe," Doyle said. "We're goin' out in the mornin' with a posse."

"And what if they are still here in town and not out there?" she asked.

"When we leave, they'll probably leave," he said. "At some point we'll give up and come back. At that point I may be able to track them from here."

"You're that good at your job?"

"Usually. It's often not how fresh a set of tracks are, as it is where they're goin'."

"Do you know who the other two are?"

"One goes by a lot of names—Dave Middleton, for one—but he's usin' 'Hank Shepherd' now."

"I don't know either of those names," she said. "And the other?"

"Roxy thinks it may be a man named Sam Dunham, a real handsome fella, from what she says."

"I don't know him either."

"She says he's the sheriff's wife's first husband. And her little girl's dad."

"Oh, that Dunham," she said. "He left town just before I came here. I ain't never seen 'im, but one of my girls says she was with him for a while. She says he was not only handsome, but damn beautiful."

"Does she still work for you?" he asked. "Maybe she's seen him around."

"Could be," Bertha said, "She's got a room on the other side of the building."

"What's her name?"

"Lucy."

"I'd like to talk to her."

"Well," Bertha said, tossing the sheet off them both, "we'd have to get dressed for that."

Chapter Thirty-Three

Roxy decided to go back to Big Bertha's. Maybe one of the girls working there had seen Sam Dunham, or even Hank Shepherd."

In the saloon she went to the bar and ordered a beer. She looked around and saw three girls working the floor. There was no sign of Sam Dunham, or Big Bertha and her father.

She wondered how many people in Lincoln would know Sam Dunham if he left town years ago? She started with the bartender, but he claimed he didn't know Dunham.

"How long have you been working here?" Roxy asked the man.

"A coupla years, since Bertha opened the place."

So Bertha must have opened after Dunham left town. That meant the three girls had been working there under two years. But maybe one of them knew Dunham before that.

Roxy went to a table and waited to ask each girl separately.

* * *

Bertha led Doyle from one side of the second floor to the other.

"When I redid the floor for myself, I left some rooms on this side for my girls."

"How many girls do you have?"

"Half a dozen," Bertha said. "I work 'em three at a time, except for busy nights."

"So Lucy's in her room?"

"She should be," Bertha said. "Let's go see."

"I'll go," Doyle said. "You stay here. Which room is it?"

"End of the hall."

"I'll check it out."

"Lucy's probably seen you in here a time or two," Bertha said. "She'll know who you are."

"I'll be careful, anyway."

* * *

In one of the rooms Sam Dunham was rolling about naked on the bed with a blousy blonde. She wasn't half as beautiful as Roxy Doyle, but all he was looking for was a wet hole, and a bed for the night. For that she fit the bill.

He pinned her down and slammed his cock between her legs.

"Oh," she said, "t-that hurts."

"Shut up," he said.

"B—but that hurts!"

He started slamming in and out of her, ignoring her cries of pain.

* * *

The third girl Roxy spoke to said, "I seen a man like that. Real pretty, with a big smile. I didn't like him."

"Why not?"

"He talked mean," the girl said. "Like we didn't deserve better because we was saloon girls."

"So nobody went upstairs with him?"

"Oh yeah," the girl said. "Lucy was finishin' her shift. So she took him up to her room. I warned 'er, but she didn't listen."

"Where's her room?" Roxy asked.

"Second floor, other side."

"Thanks."

Roxy headed for the steps.

* * *

As Doyle reached the doors to the rooms, he heard a woman crying out in pain. Something was going on, but that didn't mean it was Sam Dunham.

He moved as quietly as he could. When he reached Lucy's door he listened, then knocked.

* * *

Dunham heard the knock and stopped brutalizing the girl.

"Ow!" the girl said, as he drew out of her.

"Shut up!" he hissed. "Who else is up here?"

"Lucy," the girl said.

"How many girls work here?"

"Usually six, but now we just got five."

"So one other girl's up here now?"

"You oughtta know, you came up with Lucy."

Dunham slapped her and said, "Quiet!"

He got off the bed and grabbed his gun.

* * *

Doyle heard the sound of the slap, and a girl's cry. He tried the doorknob, found the door locked, so he put his back against the wall opposite the door, and kicked out. As his heel struck the door it popped open, revealing the bloody, naked body of a girl on a bed.

At that moment the door of the room next door opened, and Sam Dunham stepped out.

* * *

When Roxy reached the other side of the second floor she saw Big Bertha, peering around a corner. When she came up behind her she startled Bertha, who turned.

"Oh, Roxy," she said.

"Where's my father?"

"Down this hall."

Roxy looked around the corner and saw her father kick open a door.

At that same moment the door next to it opened and Sam Dunham stepped out, surprising Doyle, who was staring at the dead girl.

Roxy watched as Sam Dunham shot her father.

* * *

"Dad!"

The bullet struck Gavin Doyle in the chest, knocking him down.

Roxy was so stunned by seeing her dad shot that she froze just long enough for Sam Dunham to turn, see her, and react.

Then Dunham shot Roxy Doyle.

Chapter Thirty-Four

Slowly, Roxy came awake and became aware that she was lying on her back. For a moment she didn't know where she was, thought she must have been lying on a floor, until she felt the softness of a mattress beneath her. As her eyes began to focus, she found herself staring at a white ceiling. When she moved her eyes, she saw a man staring down at her. It seemed he might have been talking to her, but she couldn't make out his words. Then, slowly, they began to make sense.

". . . Doyle, Miss Doyle, a man's voice said, "can you hear me?"

"What—where—" Roxy started to say, but her mouth was so dry she couldn't form words.

"Here you go," an older man in a white coat said, "have some water." A hand held her head up so she could take a few sips of water from a coffee mug. "Now, can you understand me?"

"Y-yes."

"I'm Doctor Edgar," the man said, "You're in my surgery."

"Surgery?"

"You were shot, Miss Doyle."

"Wha—when?"

"A couple of days ago."

Roxy tried to remember, but everything was fuzzy.

"Who-who shot me?"

"If you think you're ready to talk, the sheriff has been waiting."

"Yes, I'm ready."

"I'll bring him in."

The doctor left the room and returned with Sheriff North.

"Not long," Doctor Edgar said to North. "She needs rest."

As the lawman loomed over her she asked, "What happened?"

"You don't remember?"

"Not very much."

"According to Big Bertha, you were shot by Sam Dunham."

"Sam shot me?"

"I'm afraid so."

"Where is he?"

"He got away, and I don't know if he left town or not. I'm guessing he did."

"I'll have to find him," she said. "Is my dad looking . . . where's my dad?"

"Roxy—"

"Oh, wait," she said "I remember. Omigod! Sam shot my dad!"

"That's right."

"How is he? How's my dad?"

"Roxy . . . I'm sorry. He's dead."

"Wha—my father's . . . dead?" Hot tears filled her eyes and ran down her face.

"I'm so sorry," he said.

"I-I remember. Oh God . . ." She tried to sit up.

"Take it easy," North said, putting his hand on one shoulder. "You need to take it easy."

"I have to find Dunham!"

"You can't ride."

"How bad am I?"

"You were hit in the left shoulder. It took the doc some time to stop the bleeding."

"Where's my dad?"

"The undertaker," North said. "We didn't want to do anything until you woke and told us what you wanted."

Roxy's vision started to blur.

"I—I'm so tired . . ."

Doc Edgar came back in. Roxy heard him say, "That's enough, Sheriff."

And that was it.

* * *

Several days later Roxy stood at her father's fresh gravesite, with Sheriff and Julie North at her side, as well as Big Bertha and Gavin Doyle's other woman, Arlene. Her left shoulder was bandaged and her arm was in a sling. She couldn't ride yet, or she would have been in the saddle, searching for the man who killed her father, Sam Dunham.

As they left the graveyard Sheriff North said, "I'm goin' back out with a posse tomorrow."

"Do you have any idea where Sam is?" she asked.

"No, but I may have a line on Hank Shepherd."

"I'm coming along."

"You can't ride yet," North said. "You'll slow me down."

"I'm coming."

"Wait until the doc says you can ride," North said. "By then I may have him. If not, you can catch up."

"Where did you get the word about Hank?"

"There's a telegraph operator in town named Arnett Long. He might be getting a message from Hank within a day or so."

"The telegraph operator?"

"That's right. He's lived in town about a year and is connected to Hank."

"Why haven't you picked him up?"

"He wasn't in the office today, and he wasn't home. I'll try again in the morning."

"He's friends with them?"

"No, it seems like Long was on Hank's payroll, feeding him information about banks and payrolls, that came over the wire."

"And what about Sam?" she asked. "He must've known Sam."

"I'll find out about that."

Sheriff North left to walk his wife home and then go to his office. Big Bertha walked Roxy to the saloon, where they sat together at a table. Arlene had gone home.

The bartender brought two glasses and a bottle to the table.

"Champagne," Bertha told Roxy. "We are gonna drink a toast to Gavin Doyle."

Roxy silently accepted a glass and drank it down.

"Another glass," Roxy said. "I'm drinking to finding the man who killed him.

Chapter Thirty-Five

Roxy Doyle woke the morning after burying her father, determined to track down Sam Dunham. Failing that, she would find Hank Shepherd.

She knew Sheriff North was going to look for Arnett Long that day, but she hoped to find him first. She would not be as law abiding in her questioning.

She went directly to the telegraph office and found it locked. Next to it was a hardware store, and she went inside to ask questions.

"I don't know where Arnett is," the clerk inside said. "He should have opened by now. Maybe he overslept."

"I have a very important telegram to send," she told the clerk. "Can you tell me where he lives?"

"I probably shouldn't—"

"Oh, please . . ." Roxy said, putting her helpless female look to good use. It worked on men young and old, but especially on this young man. He gave her directions, and she thanked him and left.

* * *

Arnett Long lived in a dilapidated little house on one end of town. She approached it carefully so as not to make noise. When she knocked on the door, she heard a stirring inside.

"Come on, Arnett," she called out. "I have nothing to do with the sheriff."

The door opened a crack.

"If I talk to you or the sheriff, I'm a dead man."

"You remember who I am, don't you?"

"Yes, Ma'am."

"Then believe me when I tell you, you're a dead man if you don't talk to me," she said. "Now open the door."

He hesitated, then unlocked the door and swung it open. She stepped inside and he closed the flimsy door and locked it. He was wearing trousers, a stained shirt, and was barefoot.

"Arnett, where's Sam Dunham?" she asked.

"I don't know."

"You know who he is because I exchanged telegrams with him."

"Yes, Ma'am, but I ain't never met 'im."

"But you know Hank Shepherd."

Arnett looked down.

"Um, yeah," he said. "But if I say anythin'—"

"They're not here, Arnett, I am."

"Um, yeah . . ."

"Is he in town?"

"N-not since the bounty hunter was shot."

"Then where is he?"

"Um . . ."

"Come on!" she said. "You know where he is, so you can send him telegrams."

"The closest town with a telegraph key would be Bazeville."

"Is it a big town?"

"Not as big as Omaha or Lincoln, but growing."

"A lawman?"

"A sheriff, but . . ."

"Crooked?"

"Not exactly."

"Okay, I get it. How far is it?"

"Less than a day's ride west."

"Okay." She started for the door, then stopped and looked at him. "If you send a telegram to warn him, I'll be back. Understand?"

"I understand."

Then she turned and faced him.

"In fact, I want you to send this one . . .

* * *

Roxy left Arnett Long's house and went to the stable.

"Miss Doyle!" Woody, the hostler greeted. "I thought you'd been shot."

"I was, a few days ago," she said. "I need my horse, Woody."

"You're gonna ride?" the hostler asked. "Are you well enough?"

"Probably not, but I want the man who killed my father before New Year's Day. I don't want him to start another year."

"I understand," he said. "What about the sheriff?"

"He's going about it his way, while I go mine. Now, please, can I have my horse?"

"Yes, Ma'am. Right away."

She waited while Woody saddled her Morgan and brought it out to her.

"Here's Nona," he said.

She almost smiled.

"I hate that name."

"Good luck."

"Please, if the sheriff asks, don't tell him where I went," she said. "I want to do this myself."

"That'll be easy," Woody said. "I don't know."

Chapter Thirty-Six

On her way out of town, Roxy ran across Sheriff North, crossing the street.

"You shouldn't be on a horse yet," he said.

"It's my responsibility," she told him. "I can't just sit in town and wait."

"What do you think you're gonna find?" he asked.

"More than if I just stay in town," she said.

"Well, let me know how you do," he said. "If I'm not here when you get back, you'll know I took the posse out."

"Good luck," she said.

"To you, too."

She knew he was watching her ride out. She hoped he didn't manage to get her destination out of Arnett Long. She wanted Sam Dunham all to herself.

* * *

When she reached Bazeville later that day, every muscle in her body ached, especially her left shoulder. She found the livery and left her Morgan in the hostler's care, not making the connection she did with Woody.

This man was much older and past the age a woman like Lady Gunsmith would have on him. The look on his face remained one of boredom and pain.

She left her saddlebags at the livery and took only her rifle. She didn't know if she'd find Sam Dunham there but hoped to find Hank Shepherd. She would then make him tell her where Dunham was.

Of the two options she had—walking around town and looking for Hank, or going to the sheriff's office—she chose the second. As Arnett had told her, Bazeville was not large but was growing. It was only a few streets from the livery to the sheriff's office. Along the way she passed several saloons, none as large as Big Bertha's. When she reached the sheriff's office she knocked and entered.

A tall, rough looking man in his fifties turned and looked at her from beneath a bushy head of grey hair. He had a sheriff's star on his chest.

"Can I help you, Ma'am?"

"Sheriff, my name's Roxy Doyle."

"I know that name," he said. "I heard you were in the area. My name's Sheriff Frank Logan."

"I don't know if you heard *all* that happened, Sheriff Logan."

"Why don't you have a seat and tell me," he suggested. "You look like you're gonna fall down any minute."

"Thanks, I will."

"Can I offer you a cup of coffee? I warn you, it's pot belly coffee."

"That's fine," she said.

As she sat, he walked to the potbelly stove in the corner and poured a cup of coffee from a large, cast-iron pot.

While she sipped the hot, strong brew, she told him what had happened in Lincoln.

"I'm sorry to hear about your father," he said, when she was done. "I knew Gavin Doyle's reputation. So what brings you here?"

"The possibility that Hank Shepherd or Sam Dunham might be here."

"And you intend to . . . what? Bring them in? Or kill them? You see, I know your reputation, too."

"HOWEVER it goes will be up to them," she said. "If I can take them back, I will."

"You don't look in shape for that," he said. "It seems to have taken plenty out of you just ridin' here alone."

"I'll do what I have to do." She leaned forward and put the cup on the desk. "For now I don't suppose you know either of the men I'm looking for?"

"No, I don't," he said. "And I don't know of any strangers in town."

"You won't mind if I look around?"

"Not at all, but don't you think you need a little rest? Maybe a hotel room."

"I'm not worried about a room, right now," she said. "I'll check the saloons first. Sam Dunham is a ladies' man. He'll be where there are pretty women."

"Well, since you said he killed one in Lincoln, I hope he doesn't appeal to the women in our town."

"Oh, he will," she said. "Don't worry about that."

She stood up.

"Maybe I ought to come with you," he proposed. "You know, to catch you if you keel over."

"I'd rather do this alone," she said, "I don't want to attract any undue attention by walking in with the law."

"If you don't mind me sayin' so, Ma'am," Logan commented, "you're gonna attract attention no matter who you're with."

"Still," she said, "I appreciate the offer, but I'll go it alone."

"Suit yourself," Logan said, "but I'll be around."

Chapter Thirty-Seven

Roxy tried The Bullhead Saloon first. It was a couple of streets down from the sheriff's office, on the way back to the livery.

As she entered, it was obvious the sheriff was right. She attracted a lot of attention from the men there with her figure, her red hair, and the fact that she was a woman wearing a gun.

"What'll ya have, Miss?" a leering bartender asked.

"Beer."

"Comin' up."

The bartender drew a cold, frothy beer and set it down in front of her. She picked it up, turned her back to the bar and started studying faces.

" 'scuse me, Ma'am," a man next to her said. That beer looks a might heavy, and with a bad wing, maybe I can help?"

She looked at the man. He was young and seemed friendly, and another time and another place maybe she would have accepted.

"I don't think so," she said, "but thanks."

"My pleasure, Ma'am," he said. "You just let me know if you change your mind."

He went back to where he had come from, a table with two other men, who laughed and slapped him on the back.

Roxy scanned the room, didn't see Sam or Hank. Of course, if they had split the take from the bank, it would be foolish for them both to be in the same town, or to even be in a town this close to Lincoln. This was especially true of Dunham, since he had killed two people the night he had also shot Roxy.

Roxy had been shot before, but this was the first time she had ever been shot by a man she had slept with and had feelings for. It was odd to want to kill a man she had been so attracted to.

She sipped her beer, watched as men came and went, and finally decided to talk to one of the girls before trying another saloon.

There were two girls working the floor. Roxy moved to the end of the bar and when one girl came over with her tray to fetch drinks, she stopped her.

"Mind if I ask you a question?" she asked.

"I got a table waitin' for drinks, but, yeah, sure, go ahead."

The girl was in her twenties, pleasant looking, but not particularly pretty.

"If it'll get ya to leave," the girl went on. "With you in here, nobody's lookin' at us workin' girls."

"I'm looking for two men," Roxy said, "named Hank and Sam."

"Lots of fellas in and out of here, I don't know their names."

Roxy had seen Hank Shepherd briefly in Big Bertha's, but she had certainly seen Sam Dunham, so she described them to the girl.

"Well," the girl said, "a man that pretty I'd sure remember him. Ain't seen 'im." She picked up her tray and walked away.

She set the half-finished beer down on the bar and left the Bullhead.

Most towns had a saloon with the word "Palace" in the name. The one across the street was the Buffalo Palace. It was smaller than the Bull Head but seemed just as busy. She secured a spot at the bar and ordered a beer, put up with the stares of the men as she studied the interior. There was no sign of Hank or Sam.

There were three girls working the floor, one a bit older than the other two. Roxy chose her to question.

"I hate pretty men," the woman said. "They're too full of themselves."

"This one certainly fits the bill," Roxy agreed.

"Is he the reason your arm's in a sling?"

"He is."

"If that's the case, why bother lookin' for him?" the woman asked. "Next time he might kill you."

"Next time it's going to be a different story," Roxy explained.

"Uh-huh, well, I ain't seen such a pretty man."

"Any strangers lately?"

"Two or three," the woman said. "One over there in a corner with a blue shirt."

Roxy looked.

"That's not one of them," Roxy said, "but thanks."

"Sure. I hope you find 'im."

"Any saloons off the main street I might miss?" Roxy asked.

The woman gave her directions to two saloons: The Six Gun and Zack Wilson's.

"They're small, but if somebody was lookin' to drink and not be seen, those are your best bets."

"Thanks, again."

"I could ask the other gals for ya, if you tell me where you're stayin'."

"I just rode in, so I don't know. But you could leave a message for me with the sheriff."

"The sheriff," the woman said. "Sit over here with me a minute before you leave."

The woman led the way over to a table and they sat across from each other.

"My name's Kitty," the woman said. She looked to be in her mid-thirties with hair that used to be blonde, but now had a silver hue.

"What's on your mind?" Roxy asked.

"Not only do I dislike pretty men, but men who shoot women—although you look like you can take care of yourself."

"I can, usually," Roxy said. She looked down at her arm. "This never should've happened and was my own fault."

"Because he was so pretty?"

"Because he had just shot my father."

"Oh," she said, "I'm sorry. Dead?"

"Yes."

"And then he shot you?"

"Yes."

"I can see why you're after him."

"Why'd you want me to sit?"

Kitty looked around, then leaned forward.

"Sheriff Logan is out for himself, rather than the town. He's been wearin' a badge a long time, and it seems to be gettin' heavier."

"Sounds like a lot of lawmen."

"Did he offer to help you?"

"He did."

"He's gonna help himself first, if there's somethin' in it for him." Kitty said.

"There might be," Roxy said. "These fellas held up the bank in Lincoln, so they've got money to burn."

"You workin' with the law in Lincoln?"

"I was, but I'm on my own, now."

"I know Sheriff North and his wife," Kitty said. "Julie's a friend of mine and I like her family's bakery."

"Did you know Julie's first husband?"

"No," Kitty said, "I met her after they split up. But don't expect much from North if you go up against Logan. He ain't man enough to help. He's a gentle family man who shouldn't ought to be wearin' a badge."

"That's the impression I got."

"Logan, on the other hand, is a hard case. Just watch yourself."

They both stood up.

"Thanks for the warning," Roxy said.

Kitty picked up Roxy's half full glass and put it on her tray.

"If you don't find your man in a saloon, you'll want to try the cathouse. A blue two-story at the far end of town. It's called Maisie's."

"Thanks again."

"Come by and let me know how you make out," Kitty said. "I'd like to see a woman come out on top."

"Don't worry, I will."

Chapter Thirty-Eight

Roxy followed Kitty's directions to the Six Gun and Zack Wilson's Saloon. They were off the main street and small. It was very easy to see, upon entering, that Sam Dunham wasn't there.

Roxy had only seen Hank once, very quickly, so she couldn't tell if he was in any of the saloons, but she knew he would recognize her at first sight. She was sure that, at some point, Dunham would have described her to him. She paid close attention in every saloon and did not see any man immediately leave when she walked in, or reveal any surprise at seeing her.

After she talked to a saloon girl in each place, that left only the whorehouse, Maisie's, before she would have to try a new approach.

She found the whorehouse and studied it for a moment. The blue paint job had been done some time ago and had faded. However, the appearance of the building had little to do with what was for sale on the inside.

Roxy went to the front door, found it locked, and knocked. The woman who answered the door did not look like someone working in a whorehouse. She wore a simple, cotton, yellow dress, with a slim figure and dark hair tied in a bun. She appeared to be in her forties.

"Is this Maisie's?" Roxy asked.

"It is," the woman said. "Are you looking for some entertainment, or a job?"

"I'm looking for a couple of men, figured one or both might be here."

"A lot of men come and go, here."

"Their names are Hank Shepherd and Sam Dunham."

"We don't take names."

"Well, if there are some men here, I'd like to take a look."

"How determined are you?"

"Very."

"Which means you'd be ready to shoot my joint up."

"Definitely."

"I suppose you'd better come in, then."

Roxy entered and the woman closed the door behind her. As she turned to face Roxy, she pulled a pin out of her hair so that it fell to her shoulders, then unbuttoned the dress and peeled it off, revealing an off the shoulder, red number beneath it.

She smiled and said, "I'm Maisie, and I wish you were here for a job."

"Sorry," Roxy said, "I've got things to do. Why the dress-down?"

"It's a game we play with the local law. We're just outside the city limits, but we pretend like we're not a whorehouse."

"What are you supposed to be, instead?"

"Who cares, as long as we're not a whorehouse— even though everyone knows we are. It's a game so the local law can claim they're doing their job."

With her hair down and a smile on her face, Maisie looked younger and prettier.

"Why are you looking for these men?" she asked Roxy.

"They robbed a bank," Roxy said, then indicated her arm and added, "One of them gave me this."

"And you wanna give him the same?"

"Or worse. How many men in the place?"

"Three in the sitting room, four upstairs. You can go up and have a look," Maisie offered, "or wait for them to come down."

"Why don't we start with the sitting room?" Roxy said. "Then we can go from there."

Chapter Thirty-Nine

Maisie led Roxy to a set of double doors and slid them open. The men seated on the set of lavender divans looked up and appeared interested when they saw Roxy, even with the arm sling and the gun and holster.

"Down, boys," Maisie said, "she's not available."

The men took Maisie's word and trained their attention back on the three painted, feathered girls sitting with them.

"Any of these three?" Maisie asked.

"No," Roxy said, "none."

"What do they look like, before we go upstairs and disturb my clients?"

Roxy gave Maisie the descriptions of Hank and Sam.

"No point in going upstairs," Maisie said. "Neither one is up there."

Roxy saw something in the woman's eyes.

"But?"

"Hank," Maisie said. "I remember him."

"When?"

"He left here yesterday."

"To go where?"

"I don't know," Maisie said, "but he might have told Juliet."

"Juliet?"

"The girl he spent time with."

"But not the pretty one?"

Maisie shrugged.

"I'd still like to take a look at the men upstairs."

"You look like you need some rest. Why not stay down here and have a look when they come down. Then when they're gone you can have a talk with Juliet. Maybe your man told her something."

"He was a talker."

"I have a room you can sit in. You'll be able to see anyone who comes downstairs. Meanwhile, I can give you something to eat and drink."

"That doesn't sound bad."

"Come on."

They left the sitting room and slid the doors closed.

"This way."

Maisie took Roxy across the hall to another, smaller room, also with sliding doors. When she opened it, Roxy saw a single divan, matching the others across the way.

"This is for overflow, when we get busy."

"Do you get that busy?"

"Some nights," Maisie said. "Men come from all around to be with my girls. New Year's Eve will be a night like that. If you get your business done in the next few days, come back and you'll see."

"Maybe I will," Roxy said.

"You mean if you kill the man who shot you," Maisie said.

"I mean if I kill the man who killed my father," Roxy corrected.

"Aw, geez," Maisie said, "I had a feeling there was more to it . . . let me get you some food. Have a seat here. You'll see anyone who comes down."

And she would see if Maisie came back with anything but food.

*　*　*

When Maisie returned, she was carrying a bowl of what looked like beef stew, with a spoon in it, and a beer.

"Did you think I'd come back with something else?" Maisie asked.

"I told you," Roxy said, "Sam Dunham's a beautiful man."

"I'm a little too old to be taken in by a pretty face," Maisie said.

"I think I am, too . . . now," Roxy said, accepting the bowl. She set it down and took the beer.

"I'll sit here with you," she said. "Keep you company."

"Keep me company?" Roxy picked up the bowl and spoon and took a bite. "Wow that's the best stew I ever tasted. You must have a wonderful cook."

"Thank you."

"You cooked this?"

"Yes," Maisie said, "I love to cook."

"Why don't you have a restaurant?" Roxy asked.

"Because life doesn't always take you in the direction you want to go," Maisie said.

"I know that," Roxy said.

At that point there was the sound of people coming down the stairs. Roxy and Maisie stopped to watch.

Chapter Forty

The girl appeared at the foot of the stairs first, long and slender with long black hair. When the man came into view behind her he was a tall, rail thin man, smiling happily.

Maisie looked at Roxy, who shook her head. It was neither Hank nor Sam. Maise stood up and went out into the hall to do business.

Maisie had brought Roxy a hunk of bread, which she dipped into the stew.

When Maisie returned, Roxy was once again working on the stew with her spoon.

"Another bowl?" Maisie asked.

"No, that was fine. Thanks." She drank some of the beer but put the mug down quickly when there were footsteps on the stairs, again. This time a chubby blonde appeared, leading a small, pot-bellied man in his sixties.

"Now I know that's not him He's a regular, comes here to hide from his wife. Excuse me."

Once again Maisie went into the hall to collect, and then the blonde went off to freshen up.

There was one man left upstairs, and Roxy was hoping it would be Sam. When Maisie returned, they talked a while longer. Roxy learned that Maisie was forty and had been working in whorehouses for twenty years.

"I always hoped to have my own place, but I didn't intend for it to be a bordello. But here I am . . ."

When the third girl came down with a man, he was a thickly built fifty, and Maisie explained that he was the town blacksmith.

After Maisie collected for her girl's services, she came back to Roxy and said, "Before you leave, I'll talk to the girls and see if any of them remember anything."

"Thanks."

Angrily, Roxy dragged herself away as Maisie returned with the chubby blonde.

"None of the girls remember your pretty man, but this is Juliet. She thinks she might remember your other man.

"You said he had very dark, deep-set eyes?" the blonde asked.

"That's right."

"He didn't say his name was Hank," Juliet went on, "he told me to call him Dave. But he had eyes like that."

"He goes by a lot of names," Roxy said, her heart beating faster. "One of them is Dave Middleton."

"He didn't say his last name," Juliet said, "he just said I should call him Dave."

Roxy looked at Maisie.

"That sounds like Hank." Then she looked at the pretty blonde. "What else did he say? Anything about where he was going?"

"He said he was meetin' a friend of his for New Year's Day."

"Did he say where?"

"I'm sorry, no."

"When was he here, Juliet?"

"Yesterday."

"Tomorrow's New Year's Eve," Maisie said.

"Did he say what direction he was going?" Roxy asked.

"No," Juliet said, "just that he'd be meeting a man for a New Years celebration."

"There are two towns riding distance from here that whoop it up on New Year's Eve and Day," Maisie said.

"Where's that?" Roxy asked.

Lincoln, and Dumont."

"Well," Roxy said, "he's not going to Lincoln, that's for sure. Juliet, did he say why he was meeting this man?"

"He said somethin' about gettin' his share."

"That sounds good," Roxy said. "Thanks to you both."

"You're gonna leave now?" Maisie asked.

"How far is Dumont?" Roxy asked.

"A day's ride," Maisie said. "You could spend the night here, get a start early in the mornin, and be there by New Year's Eve."

"I could be there by morning," Roxy said.

"If your horse doesn't step in a chuckhole in the dark and break a leg, or you don't fall off. And if you do get there in time, you won't be in any shape to do what you have to do."

Roxy knew there was a chance she would fall asleep in the saddle.

"My horse . . ." she said.

"We have a barn out back. I'll have my man put the horse there. We'll have it saddled and waitin' for you in the mornin'."

"Why would you do this?" Roxy asked.

"Hey," Maisie said, "just because I never got what I wanted doesn't mean you shouldn't get what you want. And in the meantime, maybe I can convince you to come back and work for me."

"Why not?" Roxy asked. "At least I'd get to eat real good."

Chapter Forty-One

The next morning Maisie came in and woke Roxy from a deep sleep.

"Oh, Jesus, what time is it?" Roxy demanded.

"Relax, it's barely six," Maisie said. "Get dressed and come down. We'll get some food into you while we saddle your horse."

Maisie left the room. Roxy got stiffly to her feet, rubbed some life into her shoulder. She got dressed, grabbed her sling, then decided to do without it. When she came down, a bunch of the girls were having breakfast in the kitchen.

"Welcome," Juliet said. "Breakfast is served."

While they ate ham-and-eggs, Juliet introduced all the other girls.

"You're Roxy Doyle?" one of the girls said. "Lady Gunsmith?"

"That's right."

That excited most of the girls. They started asking questions until Maisie silenced them down.

"Quiet down, girls. Roxy needs to eat and get goin'. She's got somethin' to do."

They all stopped asking questions and ate.

* * *

Maisie's man's name was Chester. When she walked Roxy out behind the house to the barn, he had her Morgan saddled and ready.

"Chester, tell her the quickest route to Dumont."

Roxy listened while Chester outlined the route.

"It's a little rough, but it'll cut some of the time down. You'll be there in time for the New Year's celebration."

"You'll have to push," Maisie said. "Do you think you can make it?"

"I'll make it."

"We filled your canteen and put some food in your saddlebags."

"I don't know how to thank you."

"I told you," Maisie said. "Come back and work for me. Maybe when this is over, you'll be tired of what you've been doin'."

"You know," Roxy said, "I never would have thought I'd say this, but it's possible."

She mounted up, waved, and headed for Dumont.

* * *

Chester and Maisie were right. It was rough terrain, and after a few hours her shoulder began to throb.

She stopped several times for water, and once for some food. She hoped Dumont wouldn't be much bigger than Bazeville.

When she approached it, it was coming on dusk, and she could see the town laid out in front of her. Lights were already being lit for the night's celebrations and it seemed at least the size of Bazeville.

If Hank and Sam were there for New Year's Eve, it was likely they would be in one saloon or another. As she approached the town limits, she reined in and took the time to tuck her red hair beneath her hat. That done, she continued on into town.

She managed to ride in among the festivities without attracting too much attention. Her options were the same as Bazeville, check the saloons or stop and talk to the sheriff. This time she decided on the saloons first, not knowing what kind of a lawman she would run into.

* * *

For a town its size, Dumont had a lot of saloons. This was probably why it was a town that celebrated so much. She seemed to have half-a-dozen to choose from, and they were all brightly lit. Music filled the streets, coming from several locations.

She reined her horse in and dismounted. The center of town was lively, and she decided to simply walk among the celebrants and blend in as much as she could. She hoped the people were already drunk enough to ignore the fact that she was a woman wearing a sidearm.

When she could, she simply peered over the batwings or through the window, hoping to see Hank or Sam inside. She knew Sam Dunham was arrogant enough to believe he had made it safely away from Lincoln and was now hidden in a town filled with celebrants. He was certainly not afraid of his ex-wife's husband tracking him to this point. Roxy wondered how long it would be before Sheriff North would give up his badge.

The first two stops yielded nothing. She was able to see from outside that Hank or Sam were not inside. If she checked all the saloons in this manner and came up empty, she would have to start over and actually go inside.

Chapter Forty-Two

Roxy continued down the street, pausing to look into the saloons, but several were too large to see the entire interior from outside. By the time she reached the end of the town limits, there were three saloons she would need to go inside. They were The Palomino, The Buckboard and Balaban's Saloon.

Reversing her course, she came to The Palomino first, and went inside. The crowd was shoulder-to-shoulder, and she was jostled painfully several times as she made her way to the bar, with several "sorry sweeties" tossed her way. She allowed the incidents to pass.

When she reached the bar, she used her good arm to make room for herself. A couple of men seemed to object until they turned and looked at her. One asked if she wanted company, but she politely declined. The man shrugged and turned back to his friend.

"What'll ya have?" the bartender asked her.

"A beer."

"Champagne's on sale tonight, for New Year's," the man told her.

"Beer's fine."

"Suit yourself."

He set a cold beer in front of her.

She picked up the mug and turned to look out over the crowded interior. She was wondering if this was going to be a fruitless night. She might need to get a hotel room and then start searching the next morning when there wasn't such a crowd. Of course, waiting until morning it was possible that either man might leave town before she could spot him.

If they were going to split the proceeds of the bank job, they wouldn't be doing so in a saloon or out in the open. They would probably do it in a hotel room.

With the town as crowded as it was, it might be impossible for her to get a room for the night. And if she staked out a hotel by sitting in front, it might be the wrong one.

Knowing Sam Dunham as she did, he seemed the kind of man who would want to celebrate the holiday in a saloon, and then go to a hotel room with a woman or two. She decided to keep looking at least until midnight. Maybe the crowds would begin to thin out by then, once it was the new year.

She started to walk around the room, looking over the crowded tables, some of which had poker games going, which seemed to be private, not house games. The short time she spent with Sam Dunham, he never talked about poker, so she did not spend much time watching them.

Dunham also had never struck her as being a very friendly man, so she doubted he would be in among a group of friends. He would most likely have a girl on each arm.

As for Hank Shepherd, she had no way of knowing what his preference would be for a way to spend New Year's Eve. If he was a normal, rowdy drinker, he would be in among a crowd.

She decided not to be on the lookout for Shepherd. She kept her eyes peeled for Sam Dunham's smile and long hair. If she happened across Hank Shepherd, so be it. Dunham was the one who would stand out, even in a crowd.

A man suddenly stepped in front of her, large and drunk.

"You look like you're lookin' for company, girlie," he said.

"No thanks," she replied.

"Aw come on, girlie," he said, "it's a holiday. You don't wanna be alone."

"Actually," she said, "I do want to be alone."

Roxy didn't need any trouble, because she didn't want to attract attention. She wanted to spot Dunham, and hoped he wouldn't see her.

"I can't believe that," the big man said.

"If my man sees you bothering me," she told him, "you will believe it."

"Oh, you got a man?"

"I do," she said. "I'm just looking for him."

"Well then, maybe I can help ya. What's he look like?"

Roxy decided to answer truthfully.

"He's a real pretty fella, with long blonde hair and a pretty smile."

"A pretty fella?" the man said. "What'll you do if you find him with another gal?" He looked at her gun. "Use that?"

"I'll put a bullet into each of them."

"And then you *would* be alone and need company."

"Maybe I would."

"Well, awright!" he said, happily. "I'm gonna find your fella for ya."

"How are you going to do that?" she asked.

"I got friends all over this town," he said, "in all the saloons. If that feller's here, I'll find 'im, and then I'll find you."

Roxy decided to accept the man's assistance.

"How are you going to find me?"

"Girlie," the man said, "there ain't no other girl in this town who looks like you. I'll find ya."

And he disappeared into the crowd before she could get his name.

Chapter Forty-Three

Roxy left the Palomino after the drunk man left her, and she moved onto the Buckboard. The interior was much like that of the Palomino, crowded with happy, drunken men. Occasionally, a fight would threaten to breakout, but before it happened somebody would buy the would-be combatants a drink, and everyone was happy again.

She walked around the saloon, nursing a beer which she would never finish, fending off more offers to keep her company. As the night went on, she was afraid she would no longer be able to do that without offending some amorous drunk. Then there would be trouble, and she would start attracting attention for the wrong reasons.

As the new year approached, Roxy once again searched the smaller saloons she had checked from outside. She felt she had no choice but to go inside and look them over. It was in one of those smaller saloons that she saw him.

Hank Shepherd.

He was seated alone at a table, with a bottle of whiskey, apparently waiting for the clock to strike twelve.

Roxy crossed the room and sat across from him.

He looked at her and smiled.

"I told him this was a bad idea," he said.

"What? The bank job?"

"No," Hank said, "meetin' here, for New Year's, to split the take."

"Where is he?" she asked.

"I don't know," Hank said. "He hasn't shown up, yet."

"Tell me," Roxy asked, "whose idea was the bank robbery?"

"That was Sam's," Hank said. "He's had it in for that town for some time. He finally convinced me and sent me in to look the bank over, find out how much was in it, and recruit two more men for the job."

"Stony and Vernon."

He poured himself some whiskey, offered the bottle to her. She turned it down.

"He told me he killed your father and shot you."

"Why didn't he kill me?"

"*He's* not even sure of that," Hank said. "He said he stood over you with the gun pointed right at you, but then walked away."

"He thought that would be the end of it?"

"He said you were probably the most beautiful woman he'd ever seen. But that didn't mean he had anythin' to fear from somebody like you."

"He's going to find out he was wrong."

"He shot you once."

"He took me by surprise," she said. "Next time he sees me, it'll be face-to-face."

"You'd face him?"

"Oh yeah," she said.

"He'll probably kill you."

"I doubt it."

"Well," Hank said, "it don't matter."

"How so?"

"Because I think he's gonna stiff me," Hank said. "He probably never intended to meet me here. It was all a big job to him."

"And you're going to accept that?"

"What can I do? I'd never face him with a gun. He'd kill me for sure."

"Then tell me where he is and I'll do it for you," Roxy said.

"If I knew I'd tell you, believe me."

"I don't believe much of what you say, Hank. I'm going to turn you over to the law," she said. "I can't just let you go."

"Why not?" Hank asked. "It's Sam you want. He made a fool of you. He shot your father, and shot you. I never shot anybody. Stony killed the bank manager."

Roxy knew Hank was trying to make himself out to be innocent, with Stony and Sam taking all the blame.

"You all robbed the bank. You're all guilty of killing the bank manager."

"If you take the time to haul me back to Lincoln, you'll lose Sam. You'll never get him."

"I won't have to take you right back to Lincoln," Roxy said. "I'll turn you over to the law here. Everybody in Nebraska knows about the bank robbery and murder of the manager."

"And then what?" Hank said. "Sam's not here. I don't know where he is."

"Oh, that," Roxy said. "See, I don't believe that cowshit about him stiffing you. He's either here already, or he's coming here to meet you."

"What makes you say that?"

"Sam is a sonofabitch to women," Roxy said. "But I think you and he are friends, and he means to split with you, and you mean to split with him. Hank, I think you two are meeting here to split the money, because you have it, not him."

Hank poured himself another drink, and as he downed it somebody shouted, "Happy New Year!"

Chapter Forty-Four

Roxy couldn't find the sheriff.

The man must have been off celebrating some-where. She was sure he wouldn't respond to a shot, be-cause there were shots being fired all over town to celebrate the new year.

Hank knew he would never match Lady Gunsmith with a gun, so when she told him to put it on the table, he did. She grabbed it and tucked it into her belt.

"Let's take a walk," she said.

"Where?"

"The sheriff's office," she answered. "I spotted it as I walked around town."

"You checked all the saloons, already?" he asked, as they made their way through the crowd.

"I did."

"And you didn't see him?"

"No."

"Doesn't that convince you he's not here?" Hank asked as they stepped outside.

"No," she said. "He's in one of these saloons, or he's in a hotel room or whorehouse with a girl."

"That's what bothers you, ain't it?" Hank asked. "That he's with another girl."

"That's got nothing to do with it," she said. "I'd never be with him again, after what he's done." She gestured with her gun. "Walk that way."

The fact that she had her gun out drew no attention, because most of the men on the street had their guns in their hands.

They reached the sheriff's office and found it locked. Roxy pounded in the door, but there was no answer.

"Now what?" Hank asked.

"Well," Roxy said, "I suppose I could just shoot you and leave you in an alley. You probably wouldn't be found until morning."

Hank stared at her a moment, then said, "You wouldn't." When she didn't answer he asked, "Would you?"

"It's tempting."

* * *

As they walked away from the sheriff's office Roxy asked Hank, "Do you have a hotel room?"

"Yeah, I do. Why?"

"Because I don't think I'd be able to get one tonight. Not the way this town's jumping."

Hank's eyes bugged out.

"You wanna share a room with me?"

"Would you rather I shoot you and dump you in an alley?"

"Hell no," Hank said. "I'd be glad to share a room."

"Well," Roxy said, "that's not exactly what I had in mind."

"What did you have in mind?"

"You'll see."

* * *

Roxy woke the next morning with the early sun streaming in the window. She looked across the room to where Hank Shepherd was lying on his side, facing the wall, trussed up like a Thanksgiving turkey. She told him the night before that if he did try to turn over, she *would* shoot him. Only then she partially disrobed and slid between the sheets.

She stood up from the bed, still nursing her bandaged shoulder. Her plan that morning was to turn Hank over to the local sheriff, and continue her search for Sam Dunham, despite Hank's assurance that the man wouldn't be in town.

Chapter Forty-Five

Roxy got dressed slowly, to be sure she didn't open the stitches in her shoulder. When she was done, she walked over and nudged Hank with her foot.

"Time to get up!" she said.

She crouched down and untied his hands and feet.

"Turn over and get up," she said, standing.

Hank turned over and stood. Only then did she remove the gag.

"That wasn't a pleasant way to spend the night," he told Roxy.

"I can think of less pleasant ways," she said.

"Yeah, okay." He rubbed his wrists. "Any chance of breakfast?"

"I'm sure they'll serve you breakfast in jail."

"Great."

"Does Sam know what room you're in?"

"No," Hank said. "We were gonna meet this mornin'."

"Where?"

"In the lobby."

"What time?"

Hank shrugged.

"I was supposed to wait until he got here."

Roxy had second thoughts about turning him over to the sheriff, not knowing how good a lawman he was.

"We goin' to jail?" Hank asked.

"I think maybe we'll wait in the lobby, together."

"Does that mean there might be breakfast?" Hank asked. "There's that dining room downstairs, and we can see the lobby from there."

"Yeah, okay," she said. "Breakfast."

* * *

They got a table in the dining room, with a view of the lobby. The majority of the people there were still in a festive mood. Roxy didn't pay much attention to the food she ordered. She ate absently, barely tasting anything, as she watched for Sam Dunham to appear.

People came and went with no sign of Sam. When someone of interest did enter the lobby, it was a man wearing a badge. Roxy noticed Hank perk up at the sight of the lawman.

"Problem?" she asked.

"I don't like lawmen."

"Why not? A lot of them are crooked as they come. Maybe Sam sent this one in to check the area out."

"I—I wouldn't know anything about that."

She didn't like Hank's reaction to the lawman, it seemed to Roxy as if the outlaw knew the lawman."

Roxy's hair was flowing down over her shoulders, so anyone watching for her would pick her out easily.

When the sheriff looked into the dining room, Roxy became even more suspicious. The man started walking toward their table.

"Roxy Doyle?" he asked.

"That's right."

"I'm Sheriff Troy." He looked to be in his late thirties, surprisingly bright-eyed for the day after New Year's Eve.

"What can I do for you, Sheriff?" she asked.

"I heard you were in town," the man said, looking at Hank. "I was wonderin' if there was gonna be any trouble."

"I hope not," she said.

"Who's this?" Troy asked.

"Just a friend. We're bringing in the new year together, at breakfast."

"That right?" Troy asked Hank.

"That's right."

"How'd you know I was here, Sheriff?"

"Word got around of a beautiful redhead wearing a gun in town. I figured it could only be Lady Gunsmith. And what else could you be in town for but trouble."

"Why couldn't I just be passing through?" Roxy asked.

"I'm a lawman, Miss Doyle," Sheriff Troy said. "What else could I think?"

"You're right," she said. "Most lawmen are simple-minded."

"I'm warnin' you," Troy said. "You and your friend. This is a quiet town. I'm watchin' for trouble."

Troy turned up and left.

"Why'd you back my story?" Roxy asked.

"I told you," Hank said, chewing his ham. "I don't like lawmen."

"You could've got away."

"Not if you told him about Lincoln," Hank said. "He would've tossed me into a cell."

Roxy figured Sheriff Troy wasn't working with Hank and Sam. If he was, Hank probably wouldn't have backed her story.

They finished their breakfast with no sign of Sam Dunham.

Chapter Forty-Six

Roxy didn't like it.

By noon there was still no sign of Dunham. Hank might have been right. Sam was stiffing him and keeping the entire haul for himself.

Roxy had installed them both on a sofa in the lobby. If Dunham entered, he wouldn't see them until too late.

"Tell me something, Hank," she said.

"What?"

"That necklace that Sam had. Is it worth anything?"

"What necklace?"

"He gave me a necklace to take to Lincoln and give to his daughter," Roxy said. "It was in my room, until one of your men stole it." She didn't bother telling him that she had recovered it on the trail, and that it was now in her saddlebag.

"I don't know anything about no necklace," Hank said. "And I don't think Stony or Vernon did, either."

"Then who stole it from my room?"

"Probably the same person who stole things from the other rooms."

"The hotel manager said my room was the only one."

Hank laughed.

"He was lying. He didn't want people checking out. Somebody had been pilfering things from that hotel's rooms for days."

She knew Hank wasn't telling the truth, otherwise she wouldn't have found it on the trail. But there was still no way for her to tell whether or not it was worth anything or not. Whoever stole it probably just thought it was a shiny trinket. Did Sam really want it to go to his daughter for Christmas? It didn't sound like something the Sam Dunham Roxy had come to know would do. The necklace was still a puzzle.

"How long are we gonna wait?" Hank asked.

"You tell me."

"We could wait forever, as far as I know. I still think I'm gettin' stiffed."

"And you're going to be satisfied with that?"

"I told you," Hank said. "I ain't about to go up against Sam with a gun."

"Then tell me where he is and I'll do it for you," Roxy said.

"How's that gonna help me?" Hank asked. "I'll be in jail."

"Yeah, but Sam will be, too, if he's not dead. Either way, he won't have the money."

Hank rubbed his stubbly jaw.

"You got a point."

"Then where is he?"

"I dunno," Hank said, "but I could make a few guesses. It'd take you a while to check them all."

"I'm going to be looking for Sam Dunham for how-ever long it takes me to find him," she said. "Give it some thought."

"I will," Hank said. "And the longer I think, the longer I'll stay out of jail."

"It won't be that long," she said. "If Sam doesn't show up by tonight, I'll turn you over to the sheriff. So you've only got that long."

Hank rubbed his jaw, again.

"What if I told you I could take you to Sam?" he asked.

"Why didn't you tell me that before?"

"I was hopin' against hope he'd show. But now I don't think he will."

"So how do you know where he is?"

"You must know Sam's a talker," Hank said. "Most of the time I don't even think he knows what he's talkin' about. He's mentioned a few more towns, places where he's got girls. I've told him a woman's gonna be the death of him, but he laughs. He says he's not afraid of any woman. They're his playthings. Somehow, I don't believe that of you. If I take you to him, you just might kill 'im. And maybe you'll recover the money. It's fifty thousand dollars. Think about it, Miss Doyle. You kill Sam, and we split the money."

"That's an interesting proposition," she admitted.

"Let me get my gear from my room, and my horse, and we can get goin'. He's got to be in one of those places."

"How far from here?"

"We can check two of them before nightfall. Another one tomorrow," Hank said. "If we don't find him there, I bet there'll be a girl who'll know somethin'."

"There's no girl here?" Roxy asked.

"Maybe, but it'll take too long to find out. And he may never have been here."

Roxy thought it over. She had no intention of splitting the money with Hank. But there was no problem letting him think she might.

"All right, then, Hank," she said. "Let's get your gear."

Chapter Forty-Seven

Once they collected Hank's gear from his room, they headed for the livery stable, with Roxy carrying his rifle and pistol. They had to bang on the door to get it opened. A sleepy man appeared, rubbing his eyes.

"Jesus, I had a late night," he complained. "What time is it?"

"After noon," Roxy said. "Give us our horses and you can go back to sleep."

"That suits me," the man said.

They waited outside while the hostler saddled their animals and walked them out. That was when Roxy and the man recognized each other.

"Hey, I know you," the man said, handing Roxy her reins. "We talked in the saloon, last night."

Hank was standing by his horse, far enough away from them so that he couldn't hear them.

"I remember," Roxy said.

"Did you find your friend?"

"I didn't," Roxy said. "Not yet."

"That's odd."

"Why's that?"

The hostler kept his voice down.

"This feller you're with," he said. "I saw him with the other one, the pretty one, later in the night, after I saw you. But I didn't see you again. I thought since you're with this one, you must've found the other one."

"Is he still in town?" she asked.

"He must be. He didn't come to get his horse, and this is the only livery in town. 'Course, he could've put his horse up somewhere else."

"Like if he had a woman in town, at her house, huh?" Roxy asked.

"I suppose."

"Thanks."

"You gonna be okay?" the man asked. "Need any help?"

"I'm fine."

"Well, my name's Moose," he said. "If you need me, just call."

"Thanks, Moose," she said." Oh, by the way, Sheriff Troy, can I trust him?"

"He's a good lawman," Moose said. "If you ask 'im, he'll help ya."

"Good to know, thanks."

"Hey, are we goin'?" Hank called out.

"We're going," she said. "Mount up."

* * *

They rode down the street when Hank suddenly got a bad feeling.

"Where are we goin'?" he asked.

"The sheriff's office," Roxy said.

"What for?"

"You're lying to me," Roxy said, "just trying to get out of town."

"Whoa, whataya talkin' about?"

"You were seen in town last night with Sam," Roxy said. "I want to know if he's still here."

"Who says?" Hank demanded.

"The hostler," Roxy said. "He just told me. He says Sam's horse is still in the livery. So are you going to tell me he's not in town?"

"Okay, okay," Hank said, as they approached the sheriff's office, "let's forget the lawman."

"Where is he, Hank?"

"He's got a woman in town," Hank said. "He's at her house."

"Take me there."

"Doyle," Hank said, "after he kills you, he'll kill me."

"Not if he thinks you took me to him so he could kill me." Roxy said. "Whether he kills me, or I kill him, you come out ahead,"

"Okay, okay," Hank said. "It's at the other end of town."

They rode slowly past the sheriff's office . . .

* * *

"There," Hank said, pointing to a small house in a clearing.

"If he's not here, you're dead," Roxy said. "I won't even bother to turn you in."

"He's in there."

"Good."

She drew her gun and slammed it against the side of Hank's head, knocking him off his horse. Then she dismounted and walked toward the house. She stopped twenty feet away.

"Sam!" she called out. "Sam Dunham!"

Chapter Forty-Eight

Inside the rundown house Sam Dunham was naked in bed with Angela Cutler, the owner. She looked at him over her shoulder and scowled.

"Who the hell is that?"

"I don't know," he said, innocently.

"One of your other women who tracked you down."

Dunham withdrew his hard cock from behind her, allowing her to turn around and face him. Her big, floppy breasts were topped with large, pale nipples.

"Sam! Get out here!" Roxy called.

"You sonofabitch," Angela growled, "you can't keep your other women away from here?"

Dunham swung his legs off the bed and reached for his trousers. He slipped them on and walked to the front window.

"Well, whataya know."

"Who is it?" she asked. "Another girlfriend?"

"I'm afraid so," he said. "Only this one wants to kill me."

"That's too bad," Angela said. "I want to kill you half the time myself."

He sat to pull on his boots.

"Does that mean after I take care of her, you don't want me to come back in?" he asked.

She wrapped her arms around him from behind, flattening her breasts against his back.

"Don't be stupid," she said. "After you're done, you get your ass back in this bed."

He turned his head, smiled at her and then kissed her soundly.

"Don't worry, sweetie," he said. "This won't take long."

He stood up and strapped on his gunbelt, then put on his hat and walked to the door. He opened it, turned and threw Angela a kiss, and stepped out.

Angela ran naked to the window. She knew the saddlebags filled with bank money were beneath her bed. Whether Dunham killed the woman, or the woman killed him, Angela figured to come out ahead.

* * *

Roxy was about to shout again when the door opened, and Sam Dunham stepped out. As he closed the door behind him, Roxy saw a naked woman come to the window and look out.

Dunham took a few steps toward her and stopped.

"You're as beautiful as ever, Roxy," he said, smiling that smile of his that once made her legs weak. Now all she felt was a coldness in the pit of her stomach.

"I'm sorry I had to shoot you," he said.

"I'm sure you are," she said.

"No, really," he said. "I stood over you with my gun and could have finished you very easily. But you're just too beautiful."

"You don't have a choice this time, Sam," Roxy said. "If you don't kill me, I'm going to kill you."

Dunham's smile never slipped.

"It's your call, Roxy," he said. "I'm sorry about your father, but if you forget this, turn and walk away, I'll let you live."

"Not a chance, Sam."

Dunham shrugged and said, "Well, I gave you a chance."

Sam went for his gun, but Roxy—given a fair chance—was much faster. She drew and fired, shot him in the right shoulder. His gun went flying into the dirt as he sank to his knees.

With his hand trying to staunch the flow of blood as she walked toward him, he said, "You said you loved me."

She pointed the gun at his forehead and fired again, saying, "I lied!"

Chapter Forty-Nine

Several days later, Roxy rode up to Sheriff Lloyd and Julie North's house. When she knocked Julie opened the door.

"Roxy! You're back. How wonderful. Come in, come in."

Roxy entered and Julie closed the door.

"Lloyd's in his office."

"And Violet?"

"Now that the holidays are over, she's back in school. Can I offer you coffee? Or tea?"

"Coffee would be good."

"Have a seat."

Roxy sat at the table while Julie poured two cups and carried them over. She set one down in front of Roxy and sat across from her.

"Is it . . . over?" Julie asked, a slight catch in her voice. She may have no longer been married to Sam Dunham, but he was still Violet's father.

"Yes, it's over," Roxy said.

"He's . . . dead?"

"Yes." Roxy sipped her coffee. "I dropped the money off back at the bank."

Right after Roxy shot Sam the woman started screaming, but she screamed in earnest when Roxy took the money. She kept insisting that the money was hers, but Roxy ignored her and carried the saddlebags back to her horse.

Hank Shepherd was gone, having awakened and ridden off, but Roxy didn't care about him. She had only been concerned with making Sam Dunham pay.

"I don't know what I'll tell Violet about her father," Julie said.

"Maybe this will help," Roxy reached into her shirt and brought out the necklace. "Sam had given this to me to pass to Violet." She set it on the table.

"Is . . . is it real?" Julie asked.

"I don't know," Roxy said. "I was going to give it to her myself, but I had second thoughts. I didn't know what to tell her. I think I should leave it up to you."

"I thought it was stolen from your room?" Julie asked.

"Apparently one of Sam's men thought it was real and decided to steal it. But I found it out there lying in the snow. I still didn't know what to tell Violet, so I kept it until I could decide what to do."

Julie reached out and touched it.

"Thank you," she said. "It was my mother's. I knew that sonofabitch took it when he left. It's really not worth much. I'll figure out how to give it to her."

Roxy stood up and Julie walked her to the door.

"What now, Roxy?" she asked.

"I really don't know," Roxy said. "I've spent so many years looking for my father. At least Violet can know what happened to hers."

"Is it better for her to know?" Julie asked.

"Julie, I searched for many years, with no idea what had happened to mine. In the long run, I think it's better to know. But that'll be up to you."

Roxy walked to her horse, mounted up and rode off, with no idea where to go.

Now Available!

The Gunsmith Series
Books 1 – 366

For more information
visit: www.SpeakingVolumes.us